To: Erik Said.
02-06-2022

From:
Cheries Brown
not Love :/

"What in me is dark
Illumine, what is low raise and support,
That to the height of this great argument
I may assert eternal Providence,
And justify the ways of God to men."
—*Milton.*

ADDED UPON

A Story

By NEPHI ANDERSON

Author of "The Castle Builder,"
"A Daughter of the North,"
"John St. John," "Romance of a Missionary," etc.

*"And they who keep their first estate shall be added upon;
. . . and they who keep their second estate shall have glory
added upon their heads for ever and ever."*

Bookcraft
Salt Lake City, Utah

ISBN: 0-88494-487-5

53rd Printing, 1997

Printed in the United States of America

CONTENTS

PREFACE TO THE THIRD EDITION

A religion, to be worth while, must give satisfactory answers to the great questions of life: What am I? Whence came I? What is the object of this life? and what is my destiny? True, we walk by faith, and not by sight, but yet the eye of faith must have some light by which to see. Added Upon is an effort to give in brief an outline of "the scheme of things," "the ways of God to men" as taught by the Gospel of Christ and believed in by the Latter-day Saints; and to justify and praise these ways, by a glance along the Great Plan, from a point in the distant past to a point in the future—not so far away, it is to be hoped.

On subjects where little of a definite character is revealed, the story, of necessity, could not go into great detail. It is suggestive only; but it is hoped that the mind of the reader, illumined by the Spirit of the Lord, will be able to fill in all the details that the heart may desire, to wander at will in the garden of the Lord, and dwell in peace in the mansions of the Father.

Many have told me that when they read Added Upon, it seemed to have been written directly to them. My greatest reward is to know that the little story has touched a sympathetic chord in the hearts of the Latter-day Saints, and that it has brought to some aching hearts a little ray of hope and consolation.

Nephi Anderson.

Liverpool, November 5, 1904.

PREFACE TO THE FIFTH AND ENLARGED EDITION

This story of things past, things present, and things to come has been before the Latter-day Saints for fourteen years. During this time, it seems to have won for itself a place in their hearts and in their literature. A reviewer of the book when it was first published said that "so great and grand a subject merits a more elaborate treatment." Many since then have said the story should be "added upon," and the present enlarged edition is an attempt to meet in a small way these demands. The truths restored to the earth through "Mormonism" are capable of illimitable enlargement; and when we contemplate these glorious teachings, we are led to exclaim with the poet:

> "Wide, and more wide, the kindling bosom swells,
> As love inspires, and truth its wonders tells,
> The soul enraptured tunes the sacred lyre,
> And bids a worm of earth to heaven aspire,
> 'Mid solar systems numberless, to soar,
> The death of love and science to explore."

N.A.

Salt Lake City, Utah,
May, 1912.

FOREWORD

To appreciate *Added Upon* it is necessary to know the author, Nephi Anderson. He had a very strong appreciation of his religion and for the doctrine taught by The Church of Jesus Christ of Latter-day Saints. His writings are evidence of this belief, weaving the principles of the Gospel in such a manner as to make them appeal to the young people. Of these writings, the one that stands out most prominently, and perhaps the one which best expresses the thought which was uppermost in his mind, is *Added Upon*. The title was inspired by a passage from The Pearl of Great Price which promises that those who keep their estate in this life, having previously kept the estate in the spirit life, shall be added upon with glory, with eternal life, and with a fullness of the Father's kingdom. This book sets forth many of the beauties, in fiction form, of the great principles of the Gospel which were made known through the Prophet Joseph Smith and which mean so much to the Latter-day Saints.

Nephi Anderson also wrote many short stories and the following books: *A Young Folks' History of the Church; A Daughter of the North; Marcus King, Mormon; The Castle Builder; Piney Ridge Cottage; Story of Chester Lawrence; John St. John; The Romance of a Missionary; The Boys of Springtown;* and *Dorian*.

Nephi Anderson was born January 22, 1865, in Christiania, Norway. He came with his parents to Ogden, Utah, and during his boyhood days worked on the farm assisting his father in the painting trade. As a young man he was an active member of The Church of Jesus Christ of Latter-day Saints, active in the quorums of the priesthood, the Sunday School, and the Mutual Improvement Association.

On December 22, 1880, he married Asenath Tillotson. From this marriage there were six children born, only three of whom grew to maturity, one still living. In 1891 he was called on a mission to Norway. After his return he taught in several schools in Ogden and Brigham City, Utah; later he was appointed Superintendent of Schools in Box Elder County, Utah.

He left for another mission to England in 1904, laboring under the direction of President Heber J. Grant, as assistant editor of the *Millenial Star*. Soon after this mission his wife died, leaving three children.

In 1908 he married Maud Rebecca Symons. Shortly after this marriage he was called upon a third mission to the Central States where he acted as editor of the *Liahona* magazine. When this mission was completed, he returned to Salt Lake City and lived there the rest of his life. Six children also were born from his second marriage, five of whom are living today.

For several years he labored diligently in the interest of the Genealogical Society of Utah and edited the *Utah Genealogical and Historical Magazine*. In one of his addresses given at the Assembly Hall in Salt Lake City on October 6, 1911, he stated these prophetic words:

"In conclusion, let me suggest the future of this work. I see the records of the dead and their histories gathered from every nation under heaven to one great central library in Zion—the largest and best equipped for its particular work in the world. Branch libraries may be established in the nations, but in Zion will be the records of last resort and final authority. . . ." The September 1966 issue of *The Improvement Era* wrote about this prophecy: "These words were uttered years before microfilming was ever conceived and at a time when the young Genealogical Society of Utah was so small it could hardly compare with other better-equipped and well-established genealogical organizations. The words of Nephi Anderson, spoken 55 years ago, took on a very special meaning on June 22, 1966, when the most unique storage vault of its kind in the world—a vault that stores records from 'every nation under heaven'—was dedicated in a canyon 20 miles southeast of Salt Lake City."

Nephi Anderson was a man possessed of a lovely spirit and always had gentleness and kindness in his being and his entire makeup. He never wanted to offend or give offense in any of his labors in the Church or in his transactions. He died January 6, 1923. President George Albert Smith stated the following at his funeral:

"He might have left to his wife and children sums of money and many things that we look upon as desirable, but he has left them not large sums of money, but a name and a fame, a reputation and a knowledge of a character that is worth more than all the wealth of this world; he was known for his righteousness and his intense desire to impart of the information that the Lord had given to him for the blessings of his fellow men."

PART FIRST

"The Lord possessed me in the beginning of his way, before his works of old.

"I was set up from everlasting, from the beginning, or ever the earth was.

"When there were no depths, I was brought forth; when there were no fountains abounding with water.

"Before the mountains were settled, before the hills was I brought forth:

"While as yet he had not made the earth, nor the fields, nor the highest part of the dust of the world.

"When he prepared the heavens, I was there: when he set a compass upon the face of the depth:

"When he established the clouds above: when he strengthened the fountains of the deep:

"When he gave to the sea his decree, that the waters should not pass his commandment: when he appointed the foundations of the earth:

"Then I was by him, as one brought up with him: and I was daily his delight, rejoicing always before him."—*Prov. 8:22-30.*

ADDED UPON

———

"Where was thou when I laid the foundations of the earth? . . . When the morning stars sang together, and all the Sons of God shouted for joy?"—*Job 38:4, 7.*

The hosts of heaven—sons and daughters of God —were assembled. The many voices mingling, rose and fell in one great murmur like the rising and falling of waves about to sink to rest. Then all tumult ceased, and a perfect silence reigned.

"Listen," said one to another by his side, "Father's will is heard."

A voice thrilled the multitude. It was clear as a crystal bell, and so distinct that every ear heard, so sweet, and so full of music that every heart within its range beat with delight.

"And now, children of God," were the words, "ye have arrived at a point in this stage of your development where a change must needs take place. Living, as ye have, all this time in the presence of God, and under the control of the agencies which here exist, ye have grown from children in knowledge to your present condition. God is pleased with you—the most of you, and many of you have shown yourselves to be spirits of power, whom He will

make His future rulers. Ye have been taught many
of the laws of light and life, whereby the universe
is created and controlled. True, ye have not all
advanced alike, or along the same lines. Some have
delighted more in the harmonies of music, while
others have studied the beauties of God's surrounding works. Each hath found pleasure and profit
in something; but there is one line of knowledge
that is closed to you all. In your present spiritual
state, ye have not come in contact with the grosser
materials of existence. Your experiences have been
wholly within the compass of spiritual life, and
there is a whole world of matter, about which ye
know nothing. All things have their opposites. Ye
have partly a conception of good and evil, but the
many branches into which these two principles sub-
divide, cannot be understood by you. Again, ye all
have had the hope given you that at some time ye
would have the opportunity to become like unto
your parents, even to attain to a body of flesh and
bones, a tabernacle with which ye may pass on to
perfection, and inherit that which God inherits. If,
then, ye ever become creators and rulers, ye must
first become acquainted with the existence of properties, laws, and organization of matter other than
that which surround you in this estate.

"To be over all things, ye must have passed
through all things, and have had experience with
them. It is now the Father's pleasure to grant you
this. Ye who continue steadfast, shall be added
upon, and be permitted to enter the second estate;
and if ye abide in that, ye shall be further increased

and enlarged and be worthy of the third estate, where glory shall be added upon your heads forever and ever.

"Even now, out in space, rolls another world—with no definite form, and void; but God's Spirit is there, moving upon it, and organizing the elements. In time, it will be a fit abode for you."

The voice ceased. Majesty stood looking out upon the silent multitude. Then glad hearts could contain no more, and the children of God gave a great shout of joy. Songs of praise and gladness came from the mighty throng, and its music echoed through the realms of heaven!

Then silence fell once more. The Voice was heard again:

"Now, how, and upon what principles will your salvation, exaltation, and eternal glory be brought about? It has been decided in the councils of eternity, and I will tell you.

"When the earth is prepared, two will be sent to begin the work of begetting bodies for you. It needs be that a law be given these first parents. This law will be broken, thus bringing sin into the new world. Transgression is followed by punishment; and thus ye, when ye are born into the world, will come in contact with misery, pain, suffering, and death. Ye will have a field for the exercise of justice and mercy, love and hatred. Ye will suffer, but your suffering will be the furnace through which ye will be tested. Ye will die, and your bodies will return to the earth again. Surrounded by earthly influences, ye will sin. Then, how can ye return to the Father's presence, and regain your tabernacles? Hear the plan:

"One must be sent to the earth with power over death. He will be the Son, the only begotten in the flesh. He must be sinless, yet bear the sins of the world. Being slain, He will satisfy the eternal law of justice. He will go before and bring to pass the resurrection from the dead. He will give unto you another law, obeying which, will free you from your personal sins, and set you again on the way of eternal life. Thus will your agency still be yours, that ye may act in all things as ye will."

A faint murmer ran through the assembly.

Then spoke the Father: "Whom shall I send?"

One arose, like unto the Father—a majestic form, meek, yet noble—the Son; and thus he spoke:

"Father, here am I, send me. Thy will be done, and the glory be thine forever."

Then another arose. Erect and proud he stood. His eyes flashed, his lips curled in scorn. Bold in his bearing, brilliant and influential, Lucifer, the Son of the Morning, spoke:

"Behold I, send me. I will be thy son, and I will redeem all mankind, that not one soul shall be lost; and surely I will do it; wherefore, give me thine honor."

Then spoke one as with authority:

"Lucifer, thy plan would destroy the agency of man—his most priceless gift. It would take away his means of eternal advancement. Your offer cannot be accepted."

The Father looked out over the vast throng; then clearly the words rang out:

"I will send the first!"

But the haughty spirit yielded not. His countenance became fiercer in its anger, and as he strode from the assembly, many followed after him.

Then went the news abroad throughout heaven of the council and the Father's proposed plan; of Christ's offer, and Lucifer's rebellious actions. The whole celestial realm was agitated, and contention and strife began to wage among the children of God.

Returning from the council chamber of the celestial glance through the paths of the surrounding gardens, came two sons of God. Apparently, the late events had affected them greatly. The assembly had dispersed, and, save now and then a fleeting figure, they were alone. They were engaged in earnest conversation.

"But, Brother Sardus," said one, "how can you look at it in that light? Lucifer was surely in the wrong. And then, how haughty and overbearing he was."

"I cannot agree with you, Homan. We have a right to think and to act as we please, and I consider Lucifer in the right. Think of this magnificent offer, to bring back in glory to Father's presence, every one of His children, and that, too, without condition on their part."

"There! He, and you with him, talk about your rights to think and act as you please. Have you not that right? Have you not used it freely in refusing to listen to Father's counsel? Do not I exercise it in that I listen and agree with Him? But let me tell you, brother, what your reasoning will lead to."

"I know it—but go on."

"No, you do not; you do not seem to understand."

"Perhaps you will explain," said the other haughtily.

"Brother, be not angry. It is because of my love for you that I speak thus. It is evident that we, in that future world of experience and trial, will retain our agencies to choose between the opposites that will be presented to us. Without that privilege, we should cease to be intelligences, and become as inanimate things. How could we be proved without this power? How could we make any progress without it?"

"I grant it all."

"Then, what would Lucifer do? He would save you from the dangers of the world, whether you would or not. He would take away any need of volition or choice on our part. Do what we would, sink as deep into sin as we could, he would save us notwithstanding, without trial, without a purging process, with all our sins upon us; and in this condition we are expected to go on to perfection, and become kings and priests unto God our Father, exercising power and dominion over our fellow creatures. Think of it! Evil would reign triumphant. Celestial order would be changed to chaos."

The other said not a word. He could not answer his brother's array of arguments.

"Dear brother," continued Homan, "never before have I received such sorrow as when I saw you follow that rebellious Son of Morning. Henceforth quit his company. I fear for him and his followers."

"But he has such power over me, Homan. His eloquence seems to hold me, and his arguments certainly convince me. But I must go—and brother, come with me to the assembly which we are to hold. Many will be there from far and near. Will you come?"

"I cannot promise you, Sardus. Perhaps I may call and see what is said and done."

Then they parted.

Homan went to the gathering of which Sardus had spoken, and as had been intimated, he met many strange faces. Everywhere in the conversation, serious topics seemed to be uppermost. The singing was not as usual. The music, though always sweet, was sadder than ever before, and a discord seemed to have crept into the even flow of life's sweet strain. Homan had no desire to talk. He wandered from group to group with a smile for all. Sardus was in a heated discussion with some kindred spirits; but Homan did not join them. Under the beautiful spread of the trees and by the fountains, sat and walked companies of sons and daughters of God. Ah, they were fair to look upon, and Homan wondered at the creations of the Father. No two were alike, yet all bore an impress of the Creator, and each had an individual beauty of his own.

Strolling into an arbor of vines, Homan did not observe the fair daughter seated there until he turned to leave; and then he saw her. She seemed absorbed in thought, and her eyes rested on the shifting throngs.

"A sweet face, and a strange one," thought he, as he went up to her and spoke:

"Sister, what are you thinking about?"

She turned and looked at him, and then a pleased smile overspread her face.

"Shall I tell you?"

"Do, I beg of you. May I sit here?" He seated himself opposite.

"Yes, brother, sit. My thoughts had such a strange ending that I will tell you what they were. I have been sitting here looking at these many faces, both new and old, and studying their varied beauties; but none seems to me to answer for my ideal. So I have been taking a little from each face, putting all together to form another. I had just completed the composition, and was looking admiringly at the new form when you came and—and—"

"Drove away your picture. That I should not have done."

"No; it was not exactly that. It was so odd." She hesitated and turned away her head. Then she looked up into his face again and said: "My dream face seemed to blend with yours."

They looked at each other strangely.

"Do you often make dream pictures?" asked he.

"Yes, of late; but I sometimes think I should **not.**"

"Why?"

"Because of the many great events that are taking place around us daily which need our careful thought and consideration. I have been trying to comprehend this great plan of our Father's in regards to us. I have asked Mother many questions, and she has explained, but I cannot fully understand— only, it all seems so wonderful, and our Father is so good and great and wise;—but how could He be otherwise, having Himself come up through the school of the eternities?"

Her words were music to Homan's ear. Her voice was soft and sweet.

"Yet it is very strange. To think that we shall forget all we know,. and that our memories will fail to recall this world at all."

"Yes, it is all strange to us, but it cannot be otherwise. You see, if we knew all about what we really are and what our past has been, mortal experiences would not be the test or the school that Father intends it to be."

"That is true; but think of being shut out, even in our thoughts, from this world. And then, I hear that down on earth there will be much sin and misery and a power to tempt and lead astray. O, if we can but resist it, dear brother. What will this power be, do you know?"

"I have only my thoughts about it. I know nothing for a certainty; but fear not, something will prompt us to the right, and we have this hope that Father's Spirit will not forsake us. And above all, our Elder Brother has been accepted as an offering for all the sins we may do. He will come to us in purity, and with power to loose the bands of death. He will bring to us Father's law whereby we may overcome the world and its sin."

"You said the bands of death. What is death?"

"Death is simply the losing of our earthly tabernacles for a time. We shall be separated from them, but the promise is that our Elder Brother will be given power to raise them up again. With them again united, we shall become even as our parents are now, eternal, perfected, celestialized beings."

As they conversed, both faces shone with a soft, beautiful light. The joy within was traced on their countenances, and for some time it was too deep for words. Homan was drawn to this beautiful sister. All were pleasing to his eye, but he was unusually attracted to one who took such pleasure in talking about matters nearest his heart.

"I must be going," said she.

"May I go with you?"

"Come."

They wandered silently among the people, then out through the surrounding gardens, listening to the music. Instinctively, they clung to each other, nor bestowed more than a smile or a word on passing brother or sister.

"What do you think of Lucifer and his plan?" asked she.

"The talented Son of the Morning is in danger of being cast out if he persists in his course. As to his plan, it is this: 'If I cannot rule, I will ruin.'"

"And if he rule, it will still be ruin, it seems to me."

"True; and he is gaining power over many."

"Yes; he has talked with me. He is a bewitching person; but his fascination has something strange about it which I do not like."

"I am glad of that."

She looked quickly at him, and then they gazed again into each other's eyes.

"By what name may I call you?" he asked.

"My name is Delsa."

"Will you tell me where you live? May I come and talk with you again? It will give me much pleasure."

"Which pleasure will be mutual," said she.

They parted at the junction of two paths.

II.

"How art thou fallen from heaven, O, Lucifer, son of the morning."—*Isaiah 14:12.*

Never before in the experiences of the intelligences of heaven, had such dire events been fore-shadowed. A crisis was certainly at hand. Lucifer was fast gaining influence among the spirits — and they had their agency to follow whom they would. The revolving spirit had skill in argument; and the light-minded, the discontented, and the rebellious were won over.

To be assured eternal glory and power without an effort on their part, appealed to them as something to be desired. To be untrammeled with laws, to be free to act at pleasure, without jeopardizing their future welfare, certainly was an attractive proposition. The pleasures in the body would be of a nature hitherto unknown. Why not be free to enjoy them? Why this curb on the passions and desires? "Hail to Lucifer and his plan! We will follow him. He is in the right."

Many of the mighty and noble children of God arrayed themselves on the side of Christ, their Elder Brother, and waged war against Lucifer's pernicious doctrine. One of the foremost among them was Michael. He was unceasing in his efforts to bring all under the authority of the Father. The plan which had been proposed, and which had been accepted by the majority, had been evolved from the wisdom of past eternities. It had exalted worlds before. It had been proved wise and just. It was founded on correct principles. By it only could the spiritual creation go on in its evolution to greater and to higher things. It was the will of the Father, to whom they all owed their existence as progressive, spiritual organizations. To bow to Him was no humiliation. To honor and obey Him was their duty. To follow the First Born, Him whom the Father had chosen as mediator, was no more than a Father should request. Any other plan would lead to confusion. Thus reasoned the followers of Christ.

Then there were others, not valiant in either cause, who stood on neutral ground. Without strength of character to come out boldly, they aided neither the right nor the wrong. Weak-minded as they were, they could not be trusted, nor could Lucifer win them over.

Meanwhile, the earth, rolling in space, evolved from its chaotic state, and in time became a fit abode for the higher creations of God.

Then the crisis came. The edict went forth that for many of the sons and daughters of God the first estate was about to end, and that the second would be ushered in. Lucifer had now won over many of the hosts of heaven. These had failed to keep their first estate. Now there would be a separation.

A council was convened, and the leading spirits were summoned. All waited for the outcome in silent awe.

Then came the decision, spoken with heavenly authority:

"Ye valiant and loyal sons and daughters of God, blessed are ye for your righteousness and your faithfulness to God and His cause. Your reward is that ye shall be permitted to dwell on the new earth, and in tabernacles of flesh continue in the eternal course of progress, as has been marked out and explained to you."

Then, to the still defiant forms of Lucifer and his adherents this was said:

"Lucifer, son of the morning, thou hast withdrawn from the Father many of the children of heaven. They have their agency, and have chosen to believe thy lies. They have fallen with thee from before the face of God. Thus hast thou used the power given thee. Thou hast said in thy heart, I will exalt my throne above the stars of God. . . . I will be like the Most High! Thou hast sought to usurp power, to take a kingdom that does not belong to thee. God holds you all as in the hollow of His hand; yet He has not restrained thine agency. He has been patient and longsuffering with you. Rebellious children of heaven, the Father's bosom heaves with sorrow for you; but justice claims its own— your punishment is that you be cast out of heaven. Bodies of flesh and bones ye shall not have; but ye shall wander without tabernacles over the face of the earth. Ye shall be 'reserved in everlasting chains under darkness unto the judgment of the great day.' "

Thus went forth the decree of the Almighty, and with it the force of His power. Lucifer and many of the hosts of heaven were cast down. The whole realm was thrilled with the power of God. The celestial elements were stirred to their depths. Heaven wept over the fallen spirits, and the cry went out, "Lo, lo, he is fallen, even the Son of the Morning."

III.

"For thou lovedst me before the foundation of the world."
—*John* 17:24.

There was a calm in heaven like unto that of a summer morning after a night of storm.

Throughout the whole strife, the dark clouds of evil had been gathering. In the fierce struggle, the spirits of heaven had been storm-tossed as on two contending waves; but when Lucifer and his forces were cast out, the atmosphere became purged of its uncleanness, and a sweet peace brooded over all. Save for sorrow for the lost ones, nothing marred the perfect joy of heaven. All now looked forward to the consummation of that plan whereby they would become inhabitants of another world, fitted for their school of experience in the flesh. All prepared themselves with this end in view.

None was more grateful to his Father than Homan. In the midst of the strife, he had done what he could for what he thought was right. All his influence had been used with the wavering ones, and many were those who owed him a debt of gratitude. But his greatest reward was in the peace which dwelt within him and the joy with which he was greeted by all who knew him.

Through it all, Homan's thoughts had often been with the fair sister Delsa; and often he had sought her and talked with her. It pleased him greatly to see the earnestness and energy with which she defended the cause of the Father. He was drawn to her more than to the many others who were equally valiant. As he thought of it, its strangeness occurred to him. Why should it be so? He did not know. Delsa was fair; so were all the daughters of God. She had attained to great intelligence; so had thousands of others. Then wherein lay the secret of the power which drew him to'her?

The vastness of the spiritual world held enough for study, research, and for occupation. None needed to be idle, for there were duties to be performed, as much here as in any other sphere of action. In the Father's house are many mansions.

In the one where Delsa lived, she and Homan sat in earnest conversation. Through the opening leading to the garden appeared the stately form of Sardus. Homan sprang to meet him and greeted him joyously.

"Welcome, Brother Sardus, welcome!"

Delsa arose.

"This is Brother Sardus," said Homan, "and this is Sister Delsa."

"Welcome, brother," said she. "Come and sit with us."

"Sardus," continued Homan, "I thought you lost. I have not met you for a long time. You remember our last conversation? Sardus, what joy to know that you are on the safe side, that you did not fall with Lucifer—"

"Sh—h, that name. Dear brother, he tempted me sorely, but I overcame him."

"But we are shortly to meet him on new ground," continued Homan. "As seducing spirits, he and his followers will still fight against the anointed Son. They will not yield. Not obtaining bodies themselves, they will seek to operate through those of others."

"Now we know how temptation and sin will come into the world," said Delsa. "God grant that we may overcome these dangers again, as we once have done."

They conversed for some time; then Sardus departed to perform some duty.

"I, too, must go," said Delsa. "A company of sisters is soon to leave for earth, and I am going to say farewell to them."

"Delsa, you do not go with them? You are not leaving me?"

"No, Homan, my time is not yet."

"May we not go together?—but there—that is as Father wills. He will ordain for the best. There are nations yet to go to the earth, and we shall have our allotted time and place."

A group of persons was engaged in earnest conversations, when a messenger approached. He raised his hand for silence, and then announced:

"I come from the Father on an errand to you."

The company gave him close attention, and he continued: "It is pertaining to some of our brothers and sisters who have gone before us into earth-life. I shall have to tell you about them so that you may understand. A certain family of earth-children has fallen into evil ways. Not being very strong for the truth before they left us, their experiences in the other world have not made them stronger. This family, it seems, has become rooted in false doctrine and wrong living, so that those who come to them from us partake also of their error and unbelief of the truth. As you know, kinship and environment are powerful agencies in forming character, and it appears that none of the Father's children have so far been able to withstand the tendency to wrong which is exerted on all who come to this family."

The messenger paused and looked around on the listening group. Then he continued: "The Father bids me ask if any of you are willing to go in earth-life to this family, become kin to those weak-hearted ones—for their salvation."

There was a long pause as if all were considering the proposition. The messenger waited.

"Brother," asked one, "is there not danger that he who goes to this mission might himself come under the influence you speak of to such an extent that he also would be lost to the good, and thus make a failure of his mission?"

"In the earth-life, as here," replied the messenger, "all have their agency. It is, therefore, possible that those who take upon themselves this mission—for there must be two, male and female—to give way to the power of evil, and thus fail in their errand. But, consider this: the Father has sent me to you. He knows you, your hearts, your faithfulness, your strength. He knows whom He is asking to go into danger for the sake of saving souls. Yes, friends, the Father knows, and this ought to be enough for you."

The listeners bowed their heads as if ashamed of the doubting, fearful thought. Then in the stillness, one spoke as if to herself: "To be a savior,—to share in the work of our Elder Brother! O, think of it!" Then the speaker raised her head quickly. "May I go, may I?" she questioned eagerly.

"And I," "and I," came from others.

"Sister, you will do for one," said the messenger to her who had first spoken. "And now, we need a brother—yes, you, brother, will do." This to one who was pressing forward, asking to be chosen.

"Yes, yes," continued the messenger, as he smiled his pleasure on the company, "I see that the Father knows you all."

"But," faltered the sister who had been chosen, "what are we to do? May we not know?"

"Not wholly," was the reply. "Do you not remember what you have been taught, that a veil is drawn over the eyes of all who enter mortality, and the memory of this world is taken away; but this I may tell you, that by the power of your spiritual insight and moral strength you will be able to exert a correcting influence over your brothers and sisters in the flesh, and especially over those of your kin. Then again, when you hear the gospel of our Elder Brother preached, it will have a familiar sound to you and you will receive it gladly. Then you will become teachers to your households and a light unto your families. Again, not only to those in the flesh will you minister. Many will have passed from earth-life in ignorance of the gospel of salvation when you come. These must have the saving ordinances of the gospel performed for them, so that when they some time receive the truth, the necessary rites will have been performed. This work, also, is a part of your mission — to enter into the Temples of the Lord, male and female, each for his and her kind, and do this work."

A sister, pressing timidly forward near to him who had been chosen, took his hand, and looked pleadingly into the face of the messenger. "May not I, too, go?" she asked. "I believe I could help a little."

The messenger smiled at her, seeing to whose hand she clung. "I think so," he said; "but we shall see."

"When do we go?" asked the brother.

"Not yet. Abide the will of the Father,—and peace be with you all."

He left them in awed silence. Then, presently, they began to speak to each other of the wonderful things they had heard and the call that had come to some of them.

Times and seasons, nations and peoples had come and gone. Millions of the sons and daughters of God had passed through the earthly school, and had gone on to other fields of labor, some with honor, others with dishonor. God's spiritual intelligences, in their innumerable gradations were being allotted their times and places. The scheme of things inaugurated by the Father was working out its legitimate results.

Homan's time had come for him to leave his spiritual home. He was now to take the step, which, though temporarily downward, would secure him a footing by which to climb to greater heights. Delsa was still in her first estate. So also was Sardus. They, with a company, were gathered to bid Homan farewell, and thus they spoke:

"We do not know," Homan was saying, "whether or not we shall meet on the earth. Our places and callings may be far apart, and we may never know or recognize each other until that day when we shall meet again in the mansions of our Father."

"I am thankful for one thing: I understand that a more opportune time in which to fill our probation has never been known on the earth. The Gospel exists there in its fulness, and the time of utter spiritual darkness has gone. The race is strong and can give us sound bodies. Now, if we are worthy, we shall, no doubt, secure a parentage that will give us those powers of mind and body which are needed to successfully combat the powers of evil."

It was no new doctrine to them, but they loved to dwell upon the glorious theme.

"We have been taught that we shall get that position to which our preparation here entitles us. Existence is eternal, and its various stages grade naturally into one another, like the different departments of a school."

"Some have been ordained to certain positions of trust. Father knows us all, and understands what we will do. Many of our mighty ones have already gone, and many are yet with us awaiting Father's will."

"I was once quite impatient. Everything seemed to pass so slowly, I thought; but now I see in it the wisdom of the Father. What confusion would result if too many went to the earth-life at once. The experi-

ence of those who go before are for our better reception."

"Sardus," said Homan, "I hear that you are taking
great delight in music."

"That is expressing the truth mildly, dear Homan.
Lately I can think of nothing else."

"What is your opinion of a person being so carried
away with one subject?" asked one.

"I was going to say," answered Homan, "that I
think there is danger in it. Some I know who neglect
every other duty except the cultivation of a certain
gift. I think we ought to grow into a perfectly
rounded character, cultivating all of Father's gifts to
us, but not permitting any of them to become an
object of worship."

"Remember, we take with us our various traits,"
said Delsa. "I think, Homan, your view is correct. It
is well enough to excel in one thing, but that should
not endanger our harmonious development."

"I have noticed, Delsa, that you are quite an
adept at depicting the beautiful in Father's creations."

"I?" she asked; "there is no danger of my becom-
ing a genius in that line. I do not care enough for it,
though I do a little of it."

Thus they conversed; then they sang songs. Tunes
born of heavenly melody thrilled them. After a time
they separated, and Homan would have gone his way
alone, but Delsa touched him on the arm.

"Homan, there is something I wish to tell you,"
she said. "May I walk with you?"

"Instead I will go with you," he replied.

They went on together.

"I, too, soon am going to earth," she said.

"Is it true?"

"Yes; Mother has informed me and I have been preparing for some time. Dear Homan, I am so glad, still the strange uncertainty casts a peculiar feeling over me. Oh, if we could but be classmates in the future school."

"Father may order it that way," he replied. "He knows our desires, and if they are righteous and for our good He may see that they are gratified. Do you go soon?"

"Yes; but not so soon as you. You will go before and prepare a welcome for me. Then I will come." She smiled up into his face.

"By faith we see afar," he replied.

"Yes; we live by faith," she added.

Hand in hand, they went. They spoke no more, but communed with each other through a more subtle channel of silence. Celestial melodies rang in their ears; the celestial landscape gladdened their eyes; the peace of God, their Father, was in their hearts. They walked hand in hand for the last time in this, their first estate.

PART SECOND

"Our birth is but a sleep and a forgetting;
The soul that rises with us, our life's star,
  Hath had elsewhere its setting,
    And cometh from afar.
  Not in entire forgetfulness
  And not in utter nakedness,
But trailing clouds of glory do we come
  From God who is our home."

—Wordsworth.

"Two shall be born the whole wide world apart,
And speak in different tongues and have no thought
Each of the other's being, and no heed;
And these o'er unknown seas and unknown lands
Shall cross, escaping wreck, defying death;
And all unconsciously shape every act
And bend each wandering step to this one end—
That, one day, out of darkness they shall meet
And read life's meaning in each other's eyes."

—Susan Marr Spalding

I.

How it did rain! For two long months the sky had been one unchangeable color of blue; but now the dark clouds hung low and touched the horizon at every point, dropping their long-accumulated water on the thirsty barrens, soaking the dried-up fields and meadows. The earth was thirsty, and the sky had at last taken pity. It rained all day. The water-ditches along the streets of the village ran thick and black. The housewife's tubs and buckets under the dripping eaves were overrunning. The dust was washed from the long rows of trees which lined the streets.

It rained steadily all over the valley. The creek which came from the mountains, and which distributed its waters to the town and adjacent farm-lands, was unusually muddy. Up in the canyon, just above the town, it seemed to leap over the rocks with unwonted fury, dashing its brown waters into white foam. The town below, the farms and gardens of the whole valley, depended for their existence on that small river. Through the long, hot summer its waters had been distributed into streams and sub-streams like the branches of a great tree, and had carried the life-giving element to the growing vegetation in the valley; but now it was master no more. The rain was pouring down on places which the river could not reach. No wonder the river seemed angry at such usurpation.

About two miles from town, upon the high bench-land which lay above the waters in the river, stood a hut. It was built of unhewn logs, and had a mud roof. Stretches of sagebrush desert reached in every direction from it. A few acres of cleared land lay near by, its yellow stubble drinking in the rain. A horse stood under a shed. A pile of sagebrush with ax and chopping block lay in the yard.

Evening came on and still it rained. A woman often appeared at the door of the hut, and a pale, anxious face peered out into the twilight. She looked out over the bench-land and then up to the mountains. Through the clouds which hung around their summits, she could see the peaks being covered with snow. She looked at the sky, then again along the plain. She went in, closed the door, and filled the stove from the brush-wood in the box. A little girl was sitting in the corner by the stove, with her feet resting on the hearth.

"I thought I heard old Reddy's bell," she said, looking up to her mother.

"No; I heard nothing. Poor boy, he must be wet through."

The mud roof was leaking, and pans and buckets were placed here and there to catch the water. The bed had been moved a number of times to find a dry spot, but at last two milk cans and a pail had to be placed on it. Drip, drip, rang the tins—and it still rained.

The mother went again to the door. The clang

of cowbells greeted her, and in a few minutes, a
boy drove two cows into the shed. The mother held
the door open while he came stamping into the house.
He was a boy of about fifteen, wearing a big straw
hat pressed down over his brown hair, a shabby
coat, blue overalls with a rend up one leg, ragged
shoes, but no stockings. He was wet to the skin,
and a pool of water soon accumulated on the floor
where he paused for an instant.

"Rupert, you're wet through. How long you have
been! You must get your clothes off," anxiously exclaimed his mother.

"Phew!" said he, "that's a whoopin' big rain. Say,
Mother, if we'd only had this two months ago, now,
on our dry farm, wouldn't we have raised a crop
though."

"You must get your clothes off, Rupert."

"Oh, that's nothin'. I must milk first; and say,
I guess the mud's washed off the roof by the looks of
things. I guess I'll fix it."

"Never mind now, you're so wet."

"Well, I can't get any wetter, and I'll work and
keep warm. It won't do to have the water comin' in
like this—look here, there's a mud puddle right on
Sis' back, an' she don't know it."

He laughed and went out. It was quite dark,
but the rain had nearly ceased. With his wheel-
barrow and shovel he went to a ravine close by and
obtained a load of clay, which he easily threw up on
the roof of the low "lean-to"; then he climbed up
and patched the holes. A half hour's work and it was
done.

"And now I'll milk while I'm at it," he said; which he did.

"I've kept your supper warm," said his mother, as she busied with the table. "It's turned quite cold. Why did you stay so long today?"

Rupert had changed his wet clothes, and the family was sitting around the table eating mush and milk. A small lamp threw a cheery light over the bare table and its few dishes, over the faces of mother, boy, and girl. It revealed the bed, moved back into its usual corner, shone on the cupboard with its red paint nearly worn off, and dimly lighted the few pictures hanging on the rough whitewashed wall.

It was a poor home, but the lamplight revealed no discontent in the faces around the table. True, the mother's was a little pinched and careworn, which gave the yet beautiful face a sharp expression; but the other two countenances shone with health and happiness. The girl was enjoying her supper, the bright sagebrush fire, and the story book by the side of her bowl, all at the same time. She dipped, alternately, into her bowl and into her book.

The boy was the man of that family. He had combed his hair well back, and his bright, honest face gleamed in the light. He was big and strong, hardened by constant toil, matured beyond his years by the responsibility which had been placed upon him since his father's death, now four years ago. In answer to his mother's inquiries, Rupert explained:

"You see, the cows had strayed up Dry Holler,

an' I had an awful time a findin' them. I couldn't
hear any bell, neither. Dry Holler creek is just boomin',
an' there's a big lake up there now. The water has
washed out a hole in the bank and has gone into Dry
Basin, an' it's backed up there till now it's a lake
as big as Brown's pond. As I stood and looked at
the running water an' the pond, somethin' came into
my head—somethin' I heard down town last summer.
An' Mother, *we* must do it!"

The boy was glowing with some exciting thought.
His mother looked at him while his sister neglected
both book and bowl.

"Do what, Rupert?"

"Why, we must have Dry Basin, an' I'll make
a reservoir out of it, an' we'll have water in the
summer for our land, an' it'll be just the thing. With
a little work the creek can be turned into the Basin
which'll fill up during the winter an' spring. There's
a low place which we'll have to bank up, an' the
thing's done. The ditch'll be the biggest job, but
I think we can get some help on that—but we must
have the land up in Dry Holler now before someone else think of it an' settles on it. Mother, I was just
wonderin' why someone hasn't thought of this before."

The mother was taken by surprise. She sat and
looked wonderingly at the boy as he talked. The idea
was new to her, but now she thought of it, it seemed
perfectly feasible. Work was the only thing needed;
but could she and her boy do it?

Five years ago when Mr. Ames had moved upon
the bench, he had been promised that the new canal

should come high enough to bring water to his land; but a new survey had been made which had left his farm far above the irrigation limit. Mr. Ames had died before he could move his family; and they had been compelled to remain in their temporary hut these four long, hard years. Rupert had tried to farm without water. A little wheat and alfalfa had been raised, which helped the little family to live without actual suffering.

That evening, mother and son talked late into the night. Nina listened until her eyes closed in sleep. The rain had ceased altogether, and the moon, hurrying through the breaking clouds, shone in at the little curtained window. Prayers were said, and then they retired. Peaceful sleep reigned within. Without, the moonlight illumined the mountains, shining on the caps of pearly whiteness which they had donned for the night.

II.

"He that tilleth his land shall be satisfied with bread; but he that followeth vain persons is void of understanding."— *Prov. 12:11.*

Widow Ames had homesteaded one hundred and sixty acres of government land in Dry Hollow. That was a subject for a two days' gossip in the town. There was speculation about what she wanted with a dry ravine in the hills, and many shook their heads in condemnation. However, it set some to thinking and moved one man, at least, to action. Jed Bolton, the same day that he heard of it, rode up into the hills above town. Sure enough, there was a rough shanty nearly finished; some furrows had been plowed, and every indication of settlement was present. Mr. Bolton bit his lip and used language which, if it did not grate on his own ears, could not on the only other listener, his horse.

Rupert was on the roof of his shanty, and Mr. Bolton greeted him as he rode up.

"Hello, Rupe, what're ye doin'?"

"Just finishin' my house. It looks like more rain, an' I must have the roof good an' tight."

"You're not goin' to live here?"

"Oh, yes, part of the time."

"What's that for?"

"To secure our claim. Mother's homesteaded one hundred and sixty acres of this land."

"What in the world are you goin' to do with it?"

"We'll farm some of it, of course, an' we'll find some use for another part after awhile, I guess."

Then Mr. Bolton changed his tactics. He tried to discourage the boy by telling him that it was railroad land, and even if it wasn't, his own adjacent claim took it all in anyway; Rupert did not scare, but said, "I guess not," as he went on quietly fitting and pounding.

The man had to give it up. "That Ames kid" had gotten the best of him.

This was four years ago, and wonderful changes had taken place since then. Rupert had begun work on his reservoir the spring after they had taken possession. He had a most beautiful site for one; and when the melting winter snows and spring rains filled Dry Hollow creek, most of it was turned into the Basin. It slowly spread out, filled the deep ravines, and crept up to Rupert's embankment. Then he turned the stream back into its natural channel again. Many came to look at the wonder. Some of his neighbor "dry-benchers" offered to join him and help him for a share in the water. The reservoir could be greatly enlarged, and the canal leading from it around the side-hills to the bench had yet to be dug; so Rupert and his mother accepted the offers of help and the work went on rapidly. The next year Dry Bench had water. New ground was broken and cleared. Trees were set out. There was new life on the farm, and new hopes within the hearts of Widow Ames and her children.

Dry Bench farm had undergone a change. A neat frame house stood in front of the log hut, which had been boarded and painted to match the newer part. A barn filled with hay and containing horses and cows stood at a proper distance back. A granary and a corn-crib were near. The new county road now extended along the fronting of the Ames place, and a neat fence separated the garden from the public highway. On the left was the orchard, a beautiful sight. Standing in long, symmetrical rows were peaches, apples, pears, and a dozen other varieties of fruit, now just beginning to bear. At the rear, stretching nearly to the mountains, were the grain and alfalfa fields. Neighboring farms also were greatly improved by the advent of water, but none showed such labor and care as the Ames farm. Rupert grew with the growth of his labors, until he was now a tall, muscular fellow, browned and calloused. Nina was fast outgrowing childish things and entering the young-lady period. A beautiful girl she was, and a favorite among her schoolmates. She had attended school in town for the past three winters, and her brother was talking of sending her to the high school.

Practically, Rupert was the head of the family. Always respectful to his mother, and generally consulting with her on any important matter, he nevertheless could not help seeing that everything depended on him, and that he was the master mind of Ames farm. And then the neighbors came to him for advice, and older and presumably wiser men counseled with him, and so it suggested itself to Rupert that he was the master mind of all Dry Bench besides. Everybody called him a "rustler." When he had leisure for school, he was beyond school age; so, nothing daunted, he set out to study by himself. He procured the necessary books, and went to them with an energy that made up for the lack of a teacher. Nina kept pace with him for a time, but the ungraded village school curriculum was too slow for Rupert; and when one spring the young reservoir projector appeared at the county teachers' examination and passed creditably, all, as he said "just for fun and practice," the people talked again—and elected him to the board of trustees.

A beautiful spring morning dawned on Dry

Bench. A cool breeze came from the mountains and
played with the young leaves of the orchard. The
apricots were white with blossoms, and the plums
and peaches were just bursting into masses of pink
and white. The alfalfa and wheat fields were beautifully green.   Blessed Morning, what a life pro-
moter, what a dispeller of fears and bringer of hopes
thou art!

Rupert was out early. After tossing some hay
to the horses and cows, he shouldered his shovel
and strode up the ditch, whistling as he went. His
straw hat set well back on his head. His blue
"jumper" met the blue overalls which were tucked
into a pair of heavy boots. His tune was a merry
one and rang out over the still fields and up to the
hills.

Rupert's thoughts were a mixture that morning, and flew from one thing to another: the ditch
which he was to clean and repair; the condition of
the reservoir; the meeting of the school board; the
planting of the garden; the dance at the hall in
town; the wonderful spreading properties of weeds
—so on from one subject to another, until he came
to a standstill, leaning on his shovel and looking
over his farm and down to the town, fast growing
into a city. From a hundred chimneys smoke was
beginning to come, befouling the clear air of the
valley.

"It is a beautiful sight," said he to himself.
"Six years ago and what was it? Under whose hand
has this change grown? Mine. I have done most
of the work, and I can lawfully claim most of the

credit. Then it was worthless, and just the other day I was offered five thousand dollars for the place. That's pretty good. Father couldn't have done any better."

Rupert was not given to boasting, but it did seem lately that everything he set his hand to prospered exceedingly. This had brought some self-exalting thoughts into his mind; not that he talked of them to others, but he communed with them to himself, nevertheless.

That morning, as he rested his chin on his hands that clasped the end of his shovel, such thoughts swelled the pride in his heart, and his work was left undone. The sun came suddenly from behind the peak and flooded the valley with light; still Rupert stood looking over the fields. In the distance towards the left he caught sight of a horse and buggy coming at a good pace along the new country road. He watched it drawing nearer. A lady was driving. Her horse was on its mettle this morning and the reins were tight. They were at that ugly place where the road crosses the canal—he was to repair it that morning— He awoke from his dreaming with a start, but too late; the horse shied, a wheel went into the ugly hole, and the occupant was pitched into the dry bottom of the canal. Rupert ran down the road shouting "whoa" to the horse which galloped past him. The lady scrambled up before Rupert reached her.

"Are you hurt?" he inquired.

"No—no, sir," she managed to say. She was

pale and trembling. "Can you catch my horse? I think he will stop at that barn."

"I'll get your horse, never fear; just so you're not hurt. Let me help you out of the ditch."

She held out a gloved hand and he assisted her up the bank. She was just a girl, and he could have carried her home, had it been necessary.

"Thank you, sir, but could you get my horse, please? There, he is stopping at that house."

"That is where I live. I'll bring him to you, if you will wait."

"Oh, thanks; but I can walk that far. The fall has just shaken me up a little. I shall soon get over it."

They walked down the road to the gate.

"You must come in and rest," said he, "and I'll take care of your horse." She remonstrated, but he insisted, and brought her into the kitchen where his mother was busy with breakfast. Rupert explained, and his mother instantly became solicitous. She drew a rocking chair up to the fire and with gentle force seated the stranger, continuously asking questions and exclaiming, "Too bad, too bad."

Rupert readily caught the runaway animal, and, leading him into the yard, fastened and fed him.

"Take off your hat, Miss," said Mrs. Ames, "your head'll feel easier. I know it must ache with such a knock as that. I believe you're cold, too. Put your feet on the hearth—or here, I'll open the oven door—there! You must take a cup of coffee with us. It'll warm you. You haven't had breakfast yet, I dare say."

The stranger thanked her and leaned back in the chair quite content. The fall had really shaken her severely and a pain shot, now and then, into her head. Rupert foolishly fidgeted about outside before he could make up his mind to come in. Nina now made her appearance. The coffee was poured out and the stranger was invited to sit up. Once, twice, Mrs. Ames spoke to her, but she sat perfectly still. Her face was pale, her eyes half closed.

"What's the matter, Miss?" asked the mother, looking into the girl's face.

"Mother, I believe she has fainted," said Nina.

The three bent over the still form. Mrs. Ames rubbed the cold hands, Nina became nervous, and Rupert looked down into the pale, beautiful face.

"Yes, she has fainted. It is too warm in here. We must get her in the sitting room on the sofa. Rupert, help us."

Rupert stood at a distance. The mother and Nina tried to lift her, but they failed.

"You'll have to carry her in, Rupert. Come, don't stand there as if you couldn't move. It's too close in this kitchen."

But the young fellow still hesitated. To take a strange, fair girl in his arms—such a thing he had never done—but he must do so now. He put his strong arms under her and lifted her as he would a child, and carried her into the next room, where he laid his burden on the sofa. The cool air had its effect, and she opened her eyes and smiled into the faces that were bent over her.

"Lie still, my dear," said Mrs. Ames. "You have been hurt more than you think."

"Did I faint?—yes, I must have—but I'm not hurt." She tried to rise, but with a moan she sank back on the pillow which Nina had brought.

"I'll go for the doctor," said Rupert, and off he went. When he and Doctor Chase came in an hour later, the girl was again sitting at the table with Mrs. Ames and Nina.

"I met with a slight accident down the road," she explained to the doctor. "I wasn't quite killed, you see, but these good people are trying to finish me with their kindness;" and she laughed merrily.

Her name was Miss Wilton. She was a school teacher, and was on her way to answer an advertisement of the Dry Bench trustees for a teacher. She hoped the doctor would pronounce her all right that she might continue her journey, as she understood it was not far.

"You have had a severe shaking up, Miss Wilton, but I don't think you need to postpone your journey more than a few hours," was the doctor's decision.

About noon, Rupert drove Miss Wilton's horse around to the front door and delivered it to her. With a profusion of thanks, she drove away in the direction of the chairman of the school trustees. Neither Nina nor her mother had said anything about Rupert's being on the board. Mrs. Ames had once seemed to broach the subject, but a look from Rupert was enough to check her. When the school teacher disappeared down the road, Rupert again shouldered his shovel, and this time the ugly hole where the road crossed the canal was mended. That done, he returned home, hitched a horse to his car, and drove to town.

III.

"Favour is deceitful and beauty is vain."—*Proverbs 31:30.*

Miss Virginia Wilton was engaged to teach the spring term of school at the Dry Bench schoolhouse. Why that upland strip bordering the mountains should be called "Dry Bench," Miss Wilton, at first, did not understand. If there was a garden spot in this big, ofttimes barren Western country, more beautiful than Dry Bench, she had in all her rambles failed to find it. But when the secret of the big reservoir up in the hills came to her knowledge, she wondered the more; and one member of the school board from that moment rose to a higher place in her estimation; yes, went past a long row of friends, up, shall it be said to the seat of honor?

Miss Wilton gave general satisfaction, and she was engaged for the next school year.

For one whole year, the school teacher had passed the Ames farm twice each day. She called often on Mrs. Ames, and Nina became her fast friend. During those cool May mornings and afternoons, when the sky was cloudless and the breeze came from the mountains, the young school teacher passed up and down the road and fell to looking with pleasure on the beautiful fields and orchards around her, and especially at the Ames farm the central and most flourishing of them all. Perhaps it would not be fair to analyze her thoughts too closely. She was yet young, only twenty-two—Rupert's own age; yet Miss Wilton's experiences in this world's school were greater than that of the simple young farmer's.

Had she designs on the Ames farm and its master? She had been in the place a year only. How could such thoughts arise within such a little head? How could such serious schemes brood behind such laughing lips and sparkling eyes? Strange that such should be the case, but truth is ofttimes strange.

Since the railroad had been extended through the valley, the town of Willowby had grown wonderfully. Its long, straight streets enclosing the rectangular squares, had not crept, but had sped swiftly out into the country on all sides, and especially towards the mountains, until now the Ames place was within the corporated city limits. Willowby soon became a shipping point for grain and fruits to the markets which the mining towns to the north afforded. The Ames orchard consisted of the finest fruits which commanded a high price. Yes, the property was fast making its owners rich.

Rupert Ames was a "rising young man," lacking the finished polish of a higher education, no doubt, but still, he was no "green-horn." Even Miss Wilton had to acknowledge that, when she became acquainted so that she could speak freely with him. He was a shrewd business man and knew how to invest his growing bank account. It was no secret that city lots and business property were continually being added to his possessions.

As to home life at the farm, Miss Wilton was always charmed with the kind hearted mother, the bright, cheerful Nina, and the handsome, sober head of the family. Such a beautiful spirit of harmony brooded over the place! Even within the year, the observant young woman could see signs of culture and coming wealth. The repairing of old buildings, and the erecting of the new ones; the repainting and decorating of rooms; the addition of costly pictures and furniture; the beautifying of the outside surroundings—all this was observed, and a mental note taken.

For a time Rupert Ames was quite reserved in the presence of the young school teacher. Naturally reticent, he was more than ever shy in the company of an educated lady from the East. Rupert never saw her but he thought of the day of her arrival on Dry Bench and the time when he held her in his arms. Never had he referred to the latter part of the episode, though she often talked of her peculiar introduction to them.

At the end of the first year, Miss Wilton had so far shown that she was but common flesh and blood that Rupert had been in her company to a number of socials, and they had walked from church a few times together. Dame gossip at once mated the two, and pronounced it a fine match.

Early in September they had a peach party at the Ames farm. Willowby's young folks were there, and having a good time. When the sun sank behind the hills on the other side of the valley, and the cool air came from the eastern mountains, Chinese lanterns were hung on the trees, and chairs and tables were placed on the lawn. There were cake and ice-cream and peaches—peaches of all kinds, large and small, white and yellow, juicy and dry; for this was a peach party, and everybody was supposed to eat, at least, half a dozen.

The band, with Volmer Holm as leader, furnished the music; and beautiful it was, as it echoed from the porch out over the assembly on the lawn. When the strains of a waltz floated out, a dozen couples glided softly over the velvety grass.

"That's fine music, Volmer," Rupert was saying to the bandmaster, as the music ceased.

"Do you think so? We've practiced very much since our new organization was effected. Will it do for a concert?"

"You know I'm no judge of music. I like yours, though, Volmer. What do you say about it, Miss Wilton? Mr. Holm wishes to know if his music is fit for a concert?"

"Most certainly it is," answered the young lady addressed, as she stepped up with an empty peach basket. "Mr. Holm, I understand that last piece is your own composition? If so, I must congratulate you; it is most beautiful."

"Thank you," and he bowed as he gave the signal to begin again.

"Mr. Ames, more peaches are wanted—the big yellow ones. Where shall I find them?"

"I'll get some—or, I'll go with you." He was getting quite bold. Perhaps the music had something to do with that.

He did not take the basket, but led the way out into the orchard. It was quite a distance to the right tree.

"That is beautiful music," she said. "Mr. Holm is a genius. He'll make his mark if he keeps on."

"Yes, I understand that he is going East to study. That will bring him out if there is anything in him."

There was a pause in the conversation; then Rupert remarked carefully, as if feeling his way:

"Yes, there's talent in Volmer, but he makes music his god, which I think is wrong."

"Do you think so?" she asked.

What that expression meant, it was hard to say.

"Yes, I think that no man should so drown himself in one thing that he is absolutely dead to everything else. Mr. Holm does that. Volmer worships nothing but music."

Rupert filled the basket and they sauntered back.

"A more beautiful god I cannot imagine," she said, half aloud.

Rupert turned with an inquiring look on his face, but he got nothing more from her, as she was busy with a peach. Her straw hat was tilted back on her head, and the wavy brown hair was somewhat in confusion. School teaching had not, as yet, driven the roses from her cheeks, nor the smiles from her lips. There was just enough of daylight left so that Rupert could see Miss Wilton's big eyes looking into his own. How beautiful she was!

"Mr. Ames, before we get back to the company, I wish to ask you a question. Mr. Holm has asked me to sing at his concert, and I should like to help him, if the school trustees do not object."

"Why should they, Miss Wilton?"

"Well, some people, you know, are so peculiar."

"I assure you they will not care—that is, if it will not interfere with your school duties."

"As to that, not a moment. I need no rehearsals as I am used to—that is I—you see, I will sing some old song."

Miss Wilton's speech became unusually confused, and Rupert noticed it; but just then Nina and her escort joined them, and they all went back to the lawn.

"Miss Wilton's going to sing at the concert," Volmer told Rupert later in the evening. " 'Twill be a big help. She's a regular opera singer, you know. She's been in the business. I heard her sing in Denver two years ago, and she was with a troupe that passed through here some time since. I remember her well, but of course I wouldn't say anything to her about it. No doubt she wishes to forget it all."

"What do you mean?" asked Rupert, quite fiercely.

"I mean that her company then was not of the choicest, but I believe she's all right and a good enough girl. Rupe, don't bother about that. Perhaps I shouldn't have said anything to you."

"Oh, that's all right. I'm glad you mentioned it."

Still a dull, miserable pain fastened itself in Rupert Ames' heart the rest of the evening; and even when the company had gone, and Miss Wilton had lingered and sweetly said "Good-night," and the lights were out, strange thoughts and feelings drove from his eyes the sleep that usually came peacefully to him.

Rupert Ames was in love. The fact became the central idea of his existence.

During Rupert's busy life, love affairs had not occupied much of his attention. Of course, he, in common with the rest of young mankind, thought that some day he would love some girl and make her his wife; but it was always as a far-away dream to him, connected with an angelic perfection which he always found missing in the workaday world. His wife must be a pure, perfect creature. Marriage was a sacred thing—one of the great events in a person's life. Not that these views had now changed altogether, for Miss Virginia Wilton came nearer his ideal than anyone he had yet met. Still, there was considerable of the tangible present about her. She was educated, businesslike, and a leader, and he, ambitious of attaining to something in the world, would need such a woman for his wife. But that sting which Volmer Holm had given him! His wife must be beyond suspicion. He could not afford to make a mistake, for if he did, it would be the mistake of his life. But was it a sin for a girl to sing in an opera? Certainly not. Anyway, he would not condemn her unheard—and then, he was sure he loved her. It had come to him unbidden. It was no fault of his that this girl should have come into his common life, and, seemingly, completely change it.

The autumn days passed. With the work of harvesting and marketing there was no time for social gatherings. The school teacher had changed her boarding place, and her path lay no longer past the Ames farm. So Rupert mingled his thoughts with his labors, and in time there emerged from that fusion a fixed purpose.

That fall Rupert's time as school trustee expired. At the first meeting of the new board, Miss Wilton's position was given to a male teacher. The reason given for the change was that "It takes a man to govern boys." Other reasons, however, could be heard in the undercurrent of talk.

The first Sunday after he heard of it, Rupert found Miss Wilton, and together they walked up the canyon road. It was a dull, cloudy day, and not a breath moved the odorous choke-cherry bushes which lined the dusty road. Never mind what was said and done that afternoon. 'Tis an old, old story. Between woman's smiles and tears, the man gained hope and courage, and when that evening they came down the back way through the fields and orchards, Virginia Wilton was Rupert Ames' promised wife.

IV.

"O Lord, lead me in a plain path."—*Isaiah 27:11.*

The scene shifts to a land afar off toward the north, Norway—away up into one of its mountain meadows. The landscape is a mixture of grandeur and beauty. Hills upon hills, covered with pine and fir, stretch away from the lowlands to the distant glacier-clad mountains, and patches of green meadow gleam through the dark pine depths.

The clear blue sky changes to a faint haze in the hilly distance. The gentle air is perfumed with the odor of the forest. A Sabbath stillness broods over all. The sun has swung around to the northwest, and skims along the horizon as if loth to leave such a sweet scene.

Evening was settling down on the Norwegian *saeter*, or summer herd ground. Riding along the trail through the pines appeared a young man. He was evidently not at home in the forest, as he peered anxiously through every opening. His dress and bearing indicated that he was not a woodsman nor a herder of cattle. Pausing on a knoll, he surveyed the scene around him, and took off his hat that the evening breeze might cool his face. Suddenly, there came echoing through the forest, from hill to hill, the deep notes of the *lur*. The traveler listened, and then urged his horse forward. Again and again the blast reverberated, the notes dying in low echoes on the distant hills. From another rise, the rider saw the girl who was making all this wild music. She

was standing on a high knoll. Peering down into
the forest, she recognized the traveler and welcomed
him with an attempt at a tune on her long, wooden
trumpet.

"Good evening, Hansine," said he, as his horse
scrambled up the path close by, "your *lur* made welcome music this evening."

"Good evening, Hr. Bogstad," said she, "are you
not lost?"

"I was, nearly, until I heard you calling your
cows. It is a long way up here—but the air and the
scenery are grand."

"Yes, do you think so? I don't know anything
about what they call grand scenery. I've always
lived up here, and it's work, work all the time—
but those cows are slow coming home." She lifted
her *lur* to her lips and once more made the woods
ring.

Down at the foot of the hills, where the pines
gave place to small, grassy openings, stood a group
of log huts, towards which the cows were now seen
wending.

"Come, Hr. Bogstad, I see the cows are coming
I must go down to meet them."

They went down the hill together. The lowing
cows came up to the stables, and as the herd grew
larger there was a deafening din. A girl was standing in the doorway of one of the cabins, timidly watching the noisy herd.

"Come, give the cows their salt," laughingly
shouted Hansine to her.

"And get hooked all to pieces?   Not much."

"You little coward. What good would you be on a *saeter*? What do you think, Hr. Bogstad?"

As the girl caught sight of the new arrival she started and the color came to her face. He went up to her. "How are you, Signe?" he said. "How do you like life on a *saeter*?"

"Well, I hardly know," she said, seemingly quite embarrassed.

"Oh, I'll tell you," broke in the busy Hansine, as she came with a pail full of salt. "She just goes around and looks at and talks about what she calls the beauties of nature. That she likes; but as for milking, or churning, or making cheese, well—"

Then they all laughed good naturedly.

Hansine was a large, strong girl, with round, pleasant features. She and the cows were good friends. At the sound of the *lur* every afternoon the cows turned their grazing heads towards home, and, on their arrival, each was given a pat and a handful of salt. Then they went quietly into their stalls.

It was quite late that evening before the milk had been strained into the wooden platters and placed in rows on the shelves in the milk house. Hr. Bogstad and Signe had proffered their help, but they had been ordered into the house and Signe was told to prepare the evening meal. When Hansine came in, she found the table set with the cheese, milk, butter, and black bread, while Signe and Hr. Bogstad sat by the large fireplace watching a pot of boiling cream mush.

The object of Hr. Bogstad's visit was plain enough. He had been devoting his attentions to Signe Dahl for some time, and now that he was home from college on a vacation, it was natural that he should follow her from the village up to the mountains.

Hr. Bogstad, though young, was one of the rich men of Nordal. He had lately fallen heir to a large estate. In fact, Signe's parents, with a great many more, were but tenants of young Hr. Henrik Bogstad; and although it was considered a great honor to have the attentions of such a promising young man— for, in fact, Henrik was quite exemplary in all things, and had a good name in the neighborhood—still Signe Dahl did not care for him, and was uneasy in his company. She would rather sail with some of the fisher boys on the lake than be the object of envy by her companions. But Signe's slim, graceful form, large blue eyes, clear, dimpled face, light silken hair, combined with a native grace and beauty, attracted not only the fisher boys but the "fine" Hr. Bogstad also. She was now spending a few days with her cousin Hansine in the mountains. Her limited knowledge of *saeter* life was fast being augmented under her cousin's supervision, notwithstanding Hansine's remarks about her inabilities.

The cabin wherein the three were seated was of the rudest kind, but everything was scrupulously clean. The blazing pine log cast a red light over them as they sat at the table.

"So you see nothing grand in your surroundings?" asked Hr. Bogstad of Hansine.

"How can I? I have never been far from home. Mountains and forests and lakes are all I know."

"True," said he, "and we can see grandeur and beauty by contrast only."

"But here is Signe," remarked Hansine; "she has never seen much of the world, yet you should hear her. I can never get her interested in my cows. Her mind must have been far away when she dished up the mush, for she has forgotten something."

"Oh, I beg pardon," exclaimed the forgetful girl. "Let me attend to it."

She went to the cupboard and brought out the sugar and a paper of ground cinnamon, and sprinkled a layer of each over the plates of mush. Then she pressed into the middle of each a lump of butter which soon melted into a tiny yellow pond.

"I should like to hear some of these ideas of yours," remarked the visitor to Signe, who had so far forgotten her manners as to be blowing her spoonful of mush before dipping it into the butter.

"I wish I were an artist," said she, without seeming to notice his remarks. "Ah, what pictures I would paint! I would make them so natural that you could see the pine tops wave, and smell the breath of the woods as you looked at them."

"You would put me in, standing on The Lookout blowing my *lur*, wouldn't you?"

"Certainly."

"And I have no doubt that we could hear the echoes ringing over the hills," continued Hansine, soberly.

"Never mind, you needn't make fun. Yes, Hr. Bogstad, I think we have some grand natural scenes. I often climb up on the hills, and sit and look over the pines and the shining lake down toward home. Then, sometimes, I can see the ocean like a silver ribbon, lying on the horizon. I sit up there and gaze and think, as Hansine says, nearly all night. I seem to be under a spell. You know it doesn't get dark all night now, and the air is so delicious. My thoughts go out 'Over the high mountains,' as Bjornson says, and I want to be away to hear and see what the world is and has to tell me. A kind of sweet loneliness comes over me which I cannot explain."

Hr. Bogstad had finished his dish. He, too, was under a spell—the spell of a soft, musical voice.

"Then the light in the summer," she continued. "How I have wished to go north where the sun shines the whole twenty-four hours. Have you ever seen the Midnight Sun, Hr. Bogstad?"

"No; but I have been thinking of taking a trip up there this summer, if I can get some good company to go with me. Wouldn't you—"

It was then that Signe hurriedly pushed her chair away and said: "Thanks for the food."

Next morning Signe was very busy. She washed the wooden milk basins, scalded them with juniper tea, and then scoured them with sand. She churned the butter and wanted to help with the cheese, but Hansine thought that she was not paying enough attention to their visitor, so she ordered her off to her lookout on the mountain. Hr. Bogstad would help her up the steep places; besides, he could tell her the names of the ferns and flowers, and answer the thousand and one questions which she was always asking. So, of course, they had to go.

But Signe was very quiet, and Henrik said but little. He had come to the conclusion that he truly loved this girl whose parents were among the poorest of his tenants. None other of his acquaintances, even among the higher class, charmed him as did Signe. He was old enough to marry, and she was not too young. He knew full well that if he did marry her, many of his friends would criticize; but Henrik had some of the Norseman spirit of liberty, and he did not think that a girl's humble position barred her from him. True, he had received very little encouragement from her, though her parents had looked with favor upon him. And now he was thinking of her cold indifference.

They sat down on a rocky bank, carpeted with gray reindeer moss.

They had been talking of his experiences at school. He knew her desire to finish the college education cut short by a lack of means.

"Signe, I wish you would let me do you a favor."

She thought for a moment before she asked what it was.

"Let me help you attend college. You know I am able to, besides—besides, some day you may learn to think as much of me as I do of you, and then, dear Signe—"

Signe arose. "Hr. Bogstad," she said, "I wish you would not talk like that. If you do, I shall go back to Hansine."

"Why, Signe, don't be offended. I am not jesting." He stood before her in the path, and would have taken her hand, but she drew back.

"Signe, I have thought a great deal of you for a long time. You know we have been boy and girl together. My absence at school has made no difference in me. I wish you could think a little of me, Signe."

"Hr. Bogstad, I don't believe in deceiving anyone. I am sorry that you have been thinking like that about me, because I cannot think of you other than as a friend. Let us not talk about it."

If Henrik could not talk about that nearest his heart, he would remain silent, which he did.

Signe was gathering some rare ferns and mosses when Hansine's *lur* sounded through the hills. That was the signal for them, as well as the cows, to come home.

Early the next morning Hansine's brother came up to the *saeter* to take home the week's accumulation of butter and cheese. Signe, perched on the top of the two-wheeled cart, was also going home. Hr. Bogstad, mounted on his horse, accompanied them a short distance, then rode off in another direction.

V.

"Can two walk together except they be agreed?"—*Amos* 3:3.

It was nearly noon when Signe Dahl sprang from the cart, and with her bundle under her arm, ran down the hillside into the woods, following a well-beaten trail. That was the short cut home. Hans had found her poor company during the ride, and even now, alone in the woods, the serious countenance was loth to relax. A ten minutes' walk brought her to the brow of a hill, and she sauntered down its sloping side. Signe had nearly reached home, and being doubtful of her reception there, she lingered. Then, too, she could usually amuse herself alone, for she always found some new wonder in the exhaustless beauty of her surroundings.

She threw herself on a green bank, and this is the picture which she saw: Just before her, the greensward extended down to a lake, whose waters lost themselves behind cliffs and islands and pine-clad hills. Here and there in the distance towards the north, there could be seen shining spots of water; but towards the south the hills closed in precipitously, and left room only for the outlet of the lake to pour over its rocky bed into another valley below. On the farther shore, five miles distant, a few red farm houses stood out from the plats of green — all the rest was forest and rock. The sky was filled with soft, fleecy clouds, and not a breath stirred the surface of the lake. Signe gazed towards a rocky island before her. Only the roof of the house upon it could

be seen, but from its chimney arose no smoke. That
was where Signe had been born, and had lived most
of the eighteen years of her life.   The girl walked
down the hillside to the lake and again seated herself,
this time on a rock near the edge of the water. She
took a book from her bundle and began to read;
but the text was soon embellished with marginal
sketches of rocks and bits of scenery, and then both
reading and drawing had to give place to the consideration of the pictures that came thronging into
her mind.

Hr. Bogstad had actually proposed to her—the
rich and handsome Hr. Bogstad; and she, the insig-
nificant farmer girl, had refused him, had run away
from him. Signe Dahl, she ruminated, aren't you the
most foolish child in the world? He is the owner
of miles and miles of the land about here. The hills
with their rich harvest of timber, the rivers with
their fish, and even the island in the lake, are his.
To be mistress over it all—ah, what a temptation.
If she had only loved Hr. Bogstad, if she had only
liked him; but she did neither. She could not explain
the reason, but she knew that she could not be his
wife.

How could such a man love her, anyway? Was
she really so very good looking? Signe looked down
into the still, deep water and saw her own reflection
asking the question over again. There! her face, at
least, was but a little, ordinary pink and white one.
Her eyes were of the common blue color. Her hair
—well, it was a trifle wavy and more glossy than that
of other girls, but—gluck! a stone broke her mirror

into a hundred circling waves. Signe looked up with a start. There was Hagbert standing half concealed behind a bush.

"Oh, I see you," she shouted.

He came down to the water, grinning good-naturedly.

"Well," said he, "I didn't think you were so vain as all that."

"Can't a person look at the pebbles and fish at the bottom of the lake without being vain?" and she laughed her confusion away. "Say, Hagbert, is your boat close by?"

"Yes, just down by the north landing."

"Oh, that's good. I thought I would have to wait until father came this evening to get home. You'll row me across, won't you?"

"Why certainly; but I thought you had gone to the *saeter* to stay, at least a week."

"Yes, but—but, I've come home again, you see."

"Yes, I see," and he looked oddly at her. He had also seen Hr. Bogstad set out for the mountains two days before, and now he wondered.

Hagbert fetched the boat, took in his passenger, and his strong arms soon sent the light craft to the other bank.

"A thousand thanks, Hagbert," she said, as she sprang out, and then climbed up the steep path, and watched him pull back. He was a strong, handsome fellow, too, a poor fisherman, yet somehow, she felt easier in his company than in Hr. Bogstad's.

Signe found no one at home. Her mother and the children had, no doubt, gone to the mainland to

pick blueberries; so she went out into the garden
to finish her book. She became so absorbed in her
reading that she did not see her mother's start of
surprise when they came home with their baskets full
of berries.

"Well, well, Signe, is that you? What's the matter?" exclaimed her mother.

"Nothing, Mother; only I couldn't stay up there
any longer." And that was all the explanation her
mother could get until the father came home that
evening. He was tired and a little cross. From Hans
he had heard a bit of gossip that irritated him, and
Signe saw that her secret was not wholly her own.
She feared her father.

"Signe," said he, after supper, "I can guess pretty
well why you came home so soon. I had a talk with
Hr. Bogstad before he went to the *saeter*."

The girl's heart beat rapidly, but she said nothing.

"Did he speak to you about—why did you run
away from him, girl?"

"Father, you know I don't like Hr. Bogstad. I
don't know why; he is nice and all that, but I don't
like him anyway."

"You have such nonsensical ideas!" exclaimed
the father, and he paused before her in his impatient
pacing back and forth. "He, the gentleman, the
possessor of thousands. Girl, do you know what
you are doing when you act like this? Can't you
see that we are poor; that your father is worked
to death to provide for you all? That if you would
treat him as you should, we would be lifted out of

this, and could get away from this rock-ribbed island on to some land with soil on? Our future would be secure. Can't you see it, girl? O, you little fool, for running away from such a man. Don't you know he owns us all, as it were?"

"No, Father, he does not."

"The very bread you eat and the water you drink come from his possessions."

"Still, he does not own us all. He does not own me, nor shall he as long as I feel as I do now, and as long as there is other land and other water and other air to which he can lay no claim."

It was a bold speech, but something prompted her to say it. She was aroused. The mother came to intercede, for she knew both father and daughter well.

"I tell you, girl, there shall be no more foolishness. You shall do as I want you, do you hear!"

Signe arose to go, but her father caught her forcibly by the arm.

"Sit down and listen to me," he said.

The girl began to cry, and the mother interposed: "Never mind, Father; you know it's useless to talk to her now. Let her go and milk the cow. It's getting late."

So Signe escaped with her pail into the little stable where the cow had been awaiting her for over an hour. But she was a long time milking, that evening.

VI.

"Get thee out of thy country, and from thy kindred, and from thy father's house, into a land that I will show thee."— *Gen. 12:1.*

Signe Dahl sat in the little coupe of the railroad train which was carrying her to Christiania. She was the sole occupant of the compartment, her big valise resting on the opposite seat. Out through the lowered window she looked at the flying landscape, a mingling of pine hills, waters, and green meadows. An hour ago she had boarded the train at Holmen, the nearest station to Nordal. Early that morning she had tearfully kissed them all good-by and had begun her journey to that haven of rest from old country oppressions—America. She and her mother had planned it, and the father had at last given his consent. It was all the outcome of Hr. Bogstad's persistent devotions to the family on the island in the lake.

Tiring of the scenery, Signe took from a bundle a letter. It had been handed her by the postmaster at Nordal that morning as she drove past, and was from Hr. Bogstad, who was in the North with a party of tourists. She opened it and read:

"I wrote you a letter about a week ago, describing our trip up to that time. I hope you have received it. You know I have no eye for the beautiful, but I did the best I could. You should have been along and seen it all yourself.

"And now I write you again, because, dear friend,

I have heard a rumor from home that you are going to America. It is news to me if it is true. Dear Signe, don't. Wait, at least, until I can see you again, because I have something to tell you whether you go or stay. I am coming home as fast as steam can carry me. Please, don't run off like that. Why should you? I ask myself. But there, it's only rumor. You're not going, and I'll see you again in a few days, when I shall tell you all about the rest of the trip."

A smile played on Signe's face, but it soon changed to a more sober expression. What was she to cause such a commotion in the life of a man like Hr. Bogstad? That he was in earnest she knew. And here she was running away from him. He would never see her again. How disappointed he would be! She could see him driving from the station, alighting at the ferry, springing into a boat, and skimming over to the island. Up the steep bank he climbs, and little Hakon runs down to meet him, for which he receives his usual bag of candy. Perhaps he gets to the house before he finds out. Then—?

Surely the smile has changed to a tear, for Signe has wiped one away from her cheek.

To Signe, the journey that day was made up of strange thoughts and experiences. The landscape, the stopping at the station, the coming and going of people, Hr. Bogstad's letter, the folks at home, the uncertain future,—all seemed to mingle and to form one chain of thought, which ended only when the train rolled into the glass-covered station at Christiania.

With a firm grasp on her valise, she picked her way through the crowd with its noise and bustle, and placed herself safely in the care of a hackman, who soon set her down at her lodgings.

At the steamship office she learned that the steamer was not to sail for three days. So Signe meant to see what she could of the city. It was her first visit to the capital, and perhaps her last. She would make the best of her time. She had no friends in the city, but that did not hinder her from walking out alone. In the afternoon of the second day, Signe went to the art gallery, and that was the end of her sight-seeing to other parts. She lingered among the paintings of the masters and the beautiful chiseled marble—the first she had seen—until the attendant reminded her that it was time to close.

That evening the landlady informed her that a visitor had been inquiring for her during the day, a gentleman. Who could it be? He was described, and then Signe knew that it was Hr. Bogstad. He had said that he could call again in the evening.

Signe was troubled. What should she do? He was following her, but they must not meet. It would do no good. The steamer was to sail tomorrow, and she would go on board that night. She called a carriage and was driven to the wharf. Yes, it was all right, said the steward, and she was made comfortable for the night.

Among the crowd of people that came to see

the steamer sail, Signe thought she caught sight of Hr. Bogstad elbowing through the throng to get to the ship. But he was too late. The third bell had rung, the gangplank was being withdrawn, and the vessel was slowly moving away. Signe had concealed herself among the people, but now she pressed to the railing and waved her handkerchief with the rest.

Farewell to Norway, farewell to home and native land. Signe's heart was full. All that day she sat on deck. She had no desire for food, and the crowded steerage had no attractions. So she sat, busy with her thoughts and the sights about the beautiful Christiania fjord.

Early the next morning they steamed into Christiansand, and a few hours later, the last of Norway's rocky coast sank below the waters of the North Sea.

All went well for a week. Signe had not suffered much from seasickness, but now a storm was surely coming. Sailors were busy making everything snug and tight; and the night closed in fierce and dark, with the sea spray sweeping the deck.

Signe staggered down into the dimly lighted steerage. Most of the poor emigrants had crawled into their bunks, and were rolling back and forth with each lurch of the ship. Signe sat and talked with a Danish girl, each clinging to a post.

"I don't feel like going to bed," said the girl.

"Nor I. What a night it is!"

"Do you think we shall get safely across?"

"Why, certainly," replied Signe. "You mustn't be frightened at a storm."

"I try not to be afraid, but I'm such a coward."

"Think about something pleasant, now," suggested the other. "Remember where you're going and whom you are going to meet."

The girl from Denmark had confided to Signe that she was going to join her lover in America.

The girl tried to smile, and Signe continued: "What a contrast between us. I am running away; you are going to meet someone—"

Crash! A blow struck the ship and shook it from end to end; and presently the machinery came to a full stop. Then there was hurrying of feet on deck, and they could hear the boatswain's shrill pipe, and the captain giving commands. The steerage was soon a scene of terror. Those who rushed up the stairs were met with fastened doors, and were compelled to remain below. Women screamed and prayed and raved. Then the steward came in, and informed them that there was no danger, and the scene somewhat quieted down. On further inquiry it was learned that they had collided with another ship. Some damage had been done forward, but there was no further danger. However, very few slept that night, and when morning broke, clear and beautiful, with glad hearts they rushed up into the open air.

The second class was forward. Three of the passengers had been killed and quite a number injured.

If Signe had not been so poor, and had not refused help from Hr. Bogstad, she would have taken second class passage. But now, thank God for being poor and—independent!

In another week they landed at New York, and each went her own way. Signe Dahl took the first train for Chicago.

VII.

"The Lord gave and the Lord hath taken away."—Job 1:22

The news startled the young city of Willowby from the Honorable Mayor to the newest comer in the place. The railroad company had found a shorter route to its northern main line, and it had been decided to remove, or, at least, to abandon for a time, the road running through the valley. The short cut would save fifty miles of roadbed and avoid some heavy grades, but it would leave the town of Willowby twenty-five miles from the railroad. Everybody said it would be a death-blow to the place. Petitions and propositions from the citizens to the railroad company availed nothing.

The most diresome predictions came true. After the change, the life of the young town seemed to wither away. Its business almost ceased. The speculator whose tenement houses were without roof, hurriedly closed them in, and so let them stand. Safer is the farmer, in such times. His fields will still yield the same, let stocks and values in real estate rise and fall as they will.

Alderman Rupert Ames had been attending the protracted meetings of the city council; this, with other business, kept him away from home for a week. This was the explanation which he gave to his mother when he at last came home.

"Rupert," she said to him, "you must not worry so. I see you are sick—you're as pale as death now. Is there anything the matter, my boy?"

Rupert seated himself on the sofa, resting his face in his hands, and looked into the fire. He was haggard and pale.

"Mother—yes, Mother, something's the matter but I cannot tell you, I cannot tell you."

The mother sank beside him. "Rupert, what is it, are you sick?"

"No, dear Mother, I'm not sick—only at heart." He put his arms around her neck and resting his head on her shoulder, began to sob.

It had been a long time since she had seen her boy shed tears.

"Mother," he sprang to his feet and forced himself to talk, "I must tell you. The bank has failed and—and—I have not always told you of my business transactions, Mother. I now owe more than we are worth in this world. I have been investing in real estate. I paid a big price for the Riverside Addition, and the paper I asked you to sign was a mortgage on the farm to secure a loan. Mother, I thought it was a good investment, and it would have been had the railroad remained, but now property has sunk so low that all we own will not pay my debts. And the bank has failed also—O Mother!"

"My son, do not carry on like that. If the worst comes, we still have the farm, haven't we?"

"You do not understand, Mother; our creditors can take that, too."

Then she also broke down, and at sight of her tears the son gained control of his own feelings, and tried to comfort his mother. She should never want as long as he had two strong hands with which to work, he assured her. All would be right in the end. "What I have done, I can do again, Mother; and though if it comes to the worst, it will be hard, I am young yet, and have life before me."

For an hour they sat on the sofa with their arms around each other, talking and planning; and then when they became silent, the pictures they saw in the glowing coals partook of a log house, a dreary sagebrush plain, and the building of canals and reservoirs.

The worst did come. They could, perhaps, have retained a part of Ames farm, but they decided to give up everything, pay their debts, and face the world honorably. So, before Christmas, everything had been cleared up, and Widow Ames was installed in a neat three-roomed house nearer town, for which they paid a monthly rental.

Miss Virginia Wilton was on a visit to her "folks in the East." Rupert both longed and feared for her return. In his letters he had said nothing about the change in his affairs. He would wait until her return, and then he would explain it fully to her. He had decided, for her sake, to propose to her the postponement of their marriage until spring. He would certainly be better prepared then. It would be a sacrifice on his part, but Virginia would be wise enough to see its advisability. Yes, they would counsel together, and Virginia's love would be the power to hold him up. After all, the world was not so dark with such a girl as Virginia Wilton waiting to become his wife.

The day after her return to Willowby, Rupert called on her. Mrs. Worth, the landlady, responded to his knock, and said that Virginia had gone out for the day. She was, however, to give him this note if he called.

Rupert took the paper and turned away. He would find her at some neighbor's. He carefully broke the envelope and read:

Dear Mr. Ames:

As I have accepted a position to teach in another state, I shall have to leave Willowby tomorrow. I shall be too busy to see you, and you have too much good sense to follow me. Forget the past. With kindest regards, I am, *Virginia Wilton.*

———————

Nina was married on the first of the year. Widow Ames died about two weeks after.

And so life's shifting scenes came fast to Rupert Ames; and they were costly scenes of dreariness and trial; but he did not altogether give up. Many of his friends were his friends still, and he could have drowned his sorrow in the social whirl; but he preferred to sit at home during the long winter evenings, beside his fire and shaded lamp, and forget himself in his books. He seemed to be drifting away from his former life, into a strange world of his own. He lost all interest in his surroundings. To him, the world was getting empty and barren and cold.

The former beautiful valley was a prison. The hills in which his boyhood had been spent lost all their loveliness. How foolish, anyway, he began to think, to always live in a narrow valley, and never know anything of the broad world without. Surely the soul will grow small in such conditions.

Early that spring, Rupert packed his possessions in a bundle which he tied behind the saddle on his horse and bade good-bye to his friends.

"Where are you going, Rupe?" they asked.

But his answer was always, "I don't know."

VIII.

"No chastening for the present seemeth to be joyous, but grievous: nevertheless, afterward it yieldeth the peaceable fruit of righteousness unto them that are exercised thereby."—*Heb. 12:11.*

Rupert Ames had ridden all day, resting only at noon to permit his horse to graze. As for himself, he was not tired. The long pent-up energy had begun to escape, and it seemed that he could have ridden, or walked, or in any way worked hard for a long time without need of rest. Move, move he must. He had been dormant long enough; thinking, thinking, nothing but that for months. It would have driven him mad had he not made a change. Where was he going? No one knew; Rupert himself did not know; anywhere for a change; anywhere to get away, for a time, from the scenes and remembrances of the valley and town of Willowby.

At dark he rode into a village at the mouth of a gorge. Lights gleamed from the windows. A strong breeze came from the gorge, and the trees which lined the one stony street all leaned away from the mountains. Rupert had never been in the place before, but he had heard of Windtown. Was there a hotel? he asked a passer-by. No; but they took lodgers at Smith's, up the hill. At Smith's he, therefore, put up his horse and secured supper and bed. Until late at night he walked up and down Windtown's one street, and even climbed the cliffs above the town.

Next morning he was out early, and entered the canyon as the sun began to illumine its rocky domes and cast long shafts of light across the chasm. A summer morning ride through a canyon of the Rockies is always an inspiration, but Rupert was not conscious of it. Again, at noon, he fed his horse a bag of grain, and let him crop the scanty bunch-grass on the narrow hillside. A slice of bread from his pocket, dipped into the clear stream, was his own meal. Then, out of the canyon, and up the mountain, and over the divide he went. All that afternoon he rode over a stretch of sagebrush plain. It was nearly midnight when he stopped at a mining camp. In the morning he sold his horse for

three twenty-dollar gold pieces, and with his bundle
on his back, walked to the railroad station, a distance
of seven miles.

"I want a ticket," said he to the man at the little
glass window.

"Where to?"

"To—to—well, to Chicago."

The man looked suspiciously at Rupert, and then
turned to a card hanging on the wall.

"Twenty-eight-fifty," he said.

Two of the gold pieces were shoved under the
glass, and Rupert received his ticket and his change.

In the car, he secured a seat near the window
that he might see the country. It was the same
familiar mountains and streams all that day, but the
next morning when he awoke and looked out of the
car windows, a strange sight met his gaze. In every
direction, as far as he could see, stretched the level
prairie, over which the train sped in straight lines
for miles and miles. "We must be in Kansas," he
thought. "What a sight, to see so much level land."

But what was he going to do in Chicago? To see
the world, to mingle in the crowd, to jostle with his
fellow-beings—what else, he did not know.

Chicago! What a sight to the man of the mountains! Streets, houses, people and the continuous
din and traffic of the city nearly turned his head
for a time. What an ideal place in which to lose
one's self. Rupert had a bundle no longer, but in
his pocket just fifteen dollars and ten cents. He
kept well out of the clutches of the sharpers in the
city, and lived quite comfortably for a week, seeing

the sights of the wonderful city. Then, when his money was getting low, he tried to get work, as he wished to remain longer. But Rupert was a farmer, and they were not in demand within the city limits. Outside the city, Rupert fell in with a body of travelers who were going West—walking, and riding on the trains when they had a chance. He joined them. Somehow, he had ceased to consider what his doings might lead to, and as for misgivings as to the company he was keeping, that did not trouble him. For many days there was more walking than riding. Rupert was not expert at swinging himself under the cars and hanging to the brakebeams, so he traveled with the more easy-going element, who slept in the haylofts at night and got what food they could from farmhouses, though Rupert hoarded his little store of money and usually paid for what he got. Then he lost all track of time. It must have been far into the summer when Rupert separated from his companions, and found himself at the base of the mountains. Here he spent his last cent for a loaf of bread.

That night Rupert felt a fever burning within him, and in the morning he was too weak to travel. He, therefore, lay in the hay which had served him for a bed until the sun shone in upon him; then he again tried to get out, but he trembled so that he crawled back into the loft and there lay the whole day. Towards evening he was driven out by the owner of the barn. Rupert staggered along until he came to another hayloft, which he succeeded in

reaching without being seen. All that night he
tossed in fever and suffered from the pains which
racked his body. The next day a farmer found him,
and seeing his condition, brought him some food.
Then on he went again. His mind was now in a
daze. Sometimes the mountains, the houses, and
the fences became so jumbled together that he could
not distinguish one from the other. Was he losing
his mind? Or was it but the fever? Was the end
coming?—and far from home, too—Home?—he had
no home. One place was as good as another to him.
He had no distinct recollection how he got to the
usual hayloft, nor how long he lay there. It was one
confussed mass of pains and dreams and fantastic
shapes. Then the fever must have burned out, for
he awoke one night with a clear brain. Then he
slept again.

On awakening next morning and crawling out,
he saw the sun shining on the snow-tipped peaks
of the mountians. He had dreamed during the night
of his mother and Virginia and Nina, and the dream
had impressed him deeply. His haggard face was
covered with a short beard; his clothes were dirty,
and some rents were getting large. Yes, he had
reached the bottom. He could go no further. He
was a tramp—a dirty tramp. He had got to the end
of his rope. He would reach the mountains which he
still loved, and there on some cliff he would lie down
and die. He would do it—would do it!

All that day he walked. He asked not for food.
He wanted nothing from any man. Alone he had

come into the world, alone he would leave it. His face was set and hard. Up the mountain road he went, past farmhouse and village, up, farther up, until he reached a valley that looked like one he knew, but there was no town there, nothing but a level stretch of bench-land and a stream coursing down the lower part of the valley. Groves of pines extended over the foothills up towards the peaks. Up there he would go. Under the pines his bones would lie and bleach.

He left the wagon road, and followed a trail up the side of the hill. The sun was nearing the white mountain peaks. An autumn haze hung over the valley and made the distance dim and blue. The odor from the trees greeted him, and recalled memories of the time when, full of life and hope, he had roamed his native pine-clad hills. He was nearing home, anyway. The preacher had said that dying was only going home. If there was a hereafter, it could be no worse than the present; and if death ended all, well, his bones would rest in peace in this lone place. The wolf and the coyote might devour his flesh—let them—and their night howl would be his funeral dirge.

Far up, he went into the deepest of the forest. The noise of falling waters came to him as a distant hymn. He sat on the ground to rest, before he made his last climb. Mechanically, he took from his pocket a small book, his testament—his sole remaining bit of property. He opened it, and his eyes fell on some lines which he had penciled on the margin, seemingly, years and years ago. They ran as follows:

" 'Tis sorrow builds the shining ladder up,
    Whose golden rounds are our calamities."

And the passages to which they pointed read:

"My son, despise not the chastening of the Lord, nor faint
when thou art rebuked of him; for whom the Lord loveth he
chasteneth, and scourgeth every son whom he receiveth. If ye
receive chastenings, God dealeth with you as with sons, for what
son is he whom the father chasteneth not?"

The book dropped from the reader's trembling
grasp. It was then that the Angel of Mercy said, "It
is enough," and touched the young man's heart. The
long pent-up spring burst forth, and Rupert sobbed
like a child. By a huge gray rock sheltered by the
pines, he uttered his first prayer to God. For a full
hour he prayed and wept, until a peaceful spirit over-
powered him, and he slept.

Rupert awoke with a changed heart, though he
was weak and faint. Evening was coming on and he
saw the smoke curling from the chimney of a farmhouse half a mile below. Painfully, he made his way
down to it.

A young man was feeding the cows for the night,
and Rupert went up to him, and said:

"Good evening, sir; have you any objection to my
sleeping in your barn tonight?"

The man eyed him closely. Tramps did not often
come to his out-of-the-way place.

"Do you smoke?"

"No, sir."

"Then I have no objection, though I don't like
tramps around the place."

"Thank you, sir."

The man moved off, but turned again. "Have you had any supper?" he asked.

"No; but I do not care for anything to eat, thank you."

"Strange tramp, that," said the man to himself, "not wanting anything to eat. Well, go into the shanty and warm yourself, anyway."

In the shanty, Rupert found an old stove glowing with a hot fire, by the side of which he seated himself. The night was chilly in that high altitude, and Rupert spread out his palms to the warmth. Inside the house, he heard the rattle of dishes and the voices of women. Then strains of songs floated out to him, and he became an intent listener. Soon from out the humming came two sweet voices, singing. Rupert sat as one spellbound, as the song seemed to melt into his soul:

> "O my Father, thou that dwellest
>   In the high and glorious place!
> When shall I regain thy presence,
>   And again behold thy face?
> In thy holy habitation,
>   Did my spirit once reside;
> In my first primeval childhood,
>   Was I nurtured near thy side.
>
> "For a wise and glorious purpose
>   Thou hast placed me here on earth,
> And withheld the recollection
>   Of my former friends and birth;
> Yet ofttimes a secret something
>   Whispered, You're a stranger here;
> And I felt that I had wandered
>   From a more exalted sphere.

"I had learned to call thee Father,
    Through thy Spirit from on high;
But until the Key of Knowledge
    Was restored, I knew not why.
In the heavens are parents single?
    No; the thought makes reason stare.
Truth is reason; truth eternal
    Tells me I've a mother there.

"When I leave this frail existence,
    When I lay this mortal by,
Father, mother, may I meet you
    In your royal courts on high?
Then, at length, when I've completed
    All you sent me forth to do,
With your mutual approbation
    Let me come and dwell with you."

The door opened, and a young woman came out
with a small tin pail in her hand. At sight of Rupert
she gave a startled cry and backed to the door. Just
then the young farmer passed through the shanty and
explained that it was only a "traveler" warming himself. The young woman looked steadily at Rupert.
The fire shone out from the open door of the stove,
and the light danced on the rough board walls, throwing a halo of red around the girl.

"What a sweet picture," instantly thought Rupert.

Then she slowly advanced again, and, instead of
pouring the contents of the pail into a larger dish as
was her errand, she placed it on the table by Rupert,
and said, smilingly:

"Vil you have a drink of varm milk?"

"Thank you, thank you."

Then she went back.

Warm milk! What could be more delicious?
Rupert sipped the sweet fluid. How it invigorated
him and surcharged him with new life. And given
by such hands, with such a smile. It was a glimpse
of past glories.

In the morning Rupert was asked if he wanted
a job.

"Yes," was the answer.

"Can you work on a farm?"

"I've been a farmer all my life," was the reply.
"I'm not a tramp, as you understand that term."

"Well, stay around today and I'll see what I
can do. I want some help, but I cannot pay high
wages."

"Never mind the wages," said Rupert, "we'll agree
on that after a while."

The young farmer saw that he had no common
tramp to deal with, although he looked rough and
travel-stained.

"I have been sick for the past few days," explained
Rupert, "and if you can trust me, I should like to rest
up a bit before I go to work. I'm too weak to do you
much good yet."

"That'll be all right," was the answer. "I see you
need something to eat this morning, even if you
weren't hungry last night. Come with me to the
house."

So Rupert Ames remained with the farmer and
did the chores around the house until he became
stronger, when he helped with the harder work. He
was treated kindly by them all, and it was not long
before he mingled freely with the family.

During this time Rupert realized that his right senses, as he called them, were coming back to him, and every night he thanked God in vocal prayer for his deliverance from a dark pit which seemed to have yawned before him.

The Jansons were newcomers in the West, and had much to learn about farming. Mr. Janson was a Swede who had been in the country twenty years. His wife and her cousin were from Norway, the former having been in the country long enough to become Americanized; it was two years only since the latter had emigrated from her native land, so she spoke English with a foreign accent. Her name was Signe Dahl (first name pronounced in two syllables, Sig-ne). She attracted Rupert's attention from the first. She had a complexion of pink and white, blue eyes, soft, light hair; but it was not her peculiar beauty alone that attracted him. There was something else about her, an atmosphere of peace and assurance which Rupert could feel in her presence. Naturally, she was reticent at first, but on learning to know Rupert, which she seemed to do intuitively, she talked freely with him, and even seemed pleased with his company.

Two weeks went by, and Rupert proffered to remain with Mr. Janson and help him with his harvesting. The latter gladly accepted the offer, for he had by this time learned that Rupert Ames could give him many practical lessons in farming.

The song that Rupert heard that first evening continually rang in his ears. He remembered some of the words, and, as he thought of them, strange ideas came to him. One evening they were all sitting around the fire in the living room. Rupert had been telling them some of his history, and when the conversation lagged, he asked the two cousins to sing that song about "O my Father." They readily consented.

"A most beautiful song," said Rupert at its close; "and so strange. It seems to bring me back for an instant to some former existence, if that were possible. What does it mean:

> 'In thy holy habitation,
>   Did my spirit once reside;
> In my first primeval childhood
>   Was I nurtured near thy side.'

"What does it mean?"

"Signe, you explain it," said Mr. Janson. "You know, you're a better preacher than I am."

Signe made no excuses, but went to the little bookshelf and took from it two books, her English and her Norwegian Bibles. She read for the most part from the English now, but she always had the more familiar one at hand to explain any doubtful passage.

"I vill do wat I can, Mr. Ames. I cannot read English good, so you must do de reading." She opened the book and pointed to the fourth verse of the thirty-eighth chapter of the book of Job. Rupert read:

"Where wast thou when I laid the foundation of the earth? declare, if thou hast understanding.   *   *   *   When the morning stars sang together and all the sons of God shouted for joy?"

"Yes," said the reader, "that is a great question, indeed. Where was Job? Why, he was not yet born."

"Who are de sons of God?" asked Signe.

"I suppose we—all of us, in a sense."

"Of course; and ve all shouted for joy when God He laid de foundation of de earth; so, ve must have been der, and known something about it."

"Yes, but how could we? We were not yet born."

"No; not in dis vorld; but ve lived as spiritual children of our Fader in heaven."

"I don't know about that," remarked Rupert, doubtfully.

"Of course you don't. Dat's why I tell you."

They all smiled at that. Signe again turned the leaves of her Bible. "Read here," said she.

This time it was the first chapter of St. John. He read the first fourteen verses.

"Dat vill do; now read here." She returned to the sixth chapter, sixty-second verse, and he read:

"What and if ye see the Son of man ascend up to where He was before."

She turned to another. It was the twenty-eighth verse of chapter sixteen:

"I came forth from the Father, and am come into the world: again, I leave the world and go to the Father."

Still she made him read one more, the fifth verse of the seventeenth chapter:

"And now, O Father, glorify thou me with thine own self with the glory which I had with thee before the world was."

"Now, vat does it all mean, Mr. Ames?"

"I see your point, Miss Dahl. Christ certainly existed as an intelligent being before He came to this earth—yes, even before the world was."

"Certainly; our Savior vas himself as ve. He vas born, He had a body as ve, and He also had a spirit. God is de Fader of His spirit and it existed long ago, as you said. Christ is our Elder Broder. Ve are of de same family. If He existed before de vorld, why not ve? Dat's right, isn't it?"

"But couldn't Christ have been the only one who had a pre-existence? I believe something is said in your book about the Savior being the only begotten of the Father."

"Yes, in de flesh; dat is true, but God is de Fader of all spirits who have come to dis vorld to take a body. I can find you many passages to prove it."

"Well, I have never thought of these things before, but it must be true if the Bible means what it says. That's a grand principle, Mr. Janson."

"It certainly is, Mr. Ames. Many people object to it; but I cannot see, if we are to exist in a spiritual state after we leave this body, why we could not have existed before we entered it—but Signe, here, is the preacher. Her only trouble is with the w's and th's. She can't get them right yet."

Signe smiled. "No, Mr. Ames, I'm no preacher. It's all so plain to me. De Bible says ve have a Fader in heaven, and I believe it. I also believe ve have 'a Moder der,' as de song says. I can't prove it from de book, but I just use my reason on dat."

It was a new experience for Rupert to hear a
fair lady expound such doctrine. The whole thing
charmed him, both the speaker and that which was
spoken. A new light seemed to dawn upon him.
What if this life was but a school, anyway, into which
eternal souls were being sent to be proved, to be
taught.

"Have you any other quotations on the subject?"

"Oh, yes; it is full," said she. "When you get
time read Heb. 12:9, Jer. 1:4-5, Eph. 1:3-5, and John
9:1-3. I do not remember more now."

Rupert took them down, and read them that
night before he went to bed. And each day he saw
a new horizon; and the sweet-faced Norwegian was
not the least factor in this continued change of mental
vision. "God bless her," he said to himself, "God has
sent her to me for a purpose;" and he began to add
to his prayers that he might so live that he would be
worthy of the blessings which, seemingly, were coming his way.

IX.

"Even so faith, if it hath not works, is dead, being alone."
—James 2:17.

Chamogo Valley lies on the edge of the great
arid region of America. At the time of Rupert Ames'
arrival in the valley, full crops were never certain,
and during some years, rain was so scarce that there
were no crops at all. The Chicago real estate dealer

who had sold Mr. Janson his land had not enlightened
him on this fact, and so he had already lost the
best part of two years' work by failure of crops. Rupert
Ames learned of all this from Mr. Janson, and then he
wondered why advantage was not taken of the stream
in the bottom of the valley for irrigation purposes.

One day — it was near the end of the harvest,
and they were pitting their last potatoes — Rupert
asked Mr. Janson if the adjoining lands could be
bought.

"Why, yes," was the reply. "I was offered nearly
the whole valley for a small sum, but I have all the
land I care to handle. You see, this region would be
different if we could rely on the moisture, but we can't,
and I am nearly tired of it myself. Do you want to
buy me out?" This with a laugh.

"Can you raise money enough to buy this whole
valley?" asked Rupert seriously.

"Yes; I could get it."

"Then I am going to propose something to you."

Whereupon Rupert pointed out that the rich
bench lands on each side of the river could be brought
under cultivation, and crops secured every year by
bringing the water from the stream in canals, and
watering, or irrigating them. Mr. Janson listened
with wonder at Rupert's description of Dry Bench
reservoir, and how simple it would be to construct
canals by which to water Chamogo valley.

"This valley can be made to support a good-
sized population," said Rupert. "By securing the
land and digging canals to it, and then selling it out

in farms again—well, if you don't make a hundred per cent on your investment, I am mistaken."

They had many talks on the scheme, and at last it was decided to try it. Rupert would supervise the construction of the canals. He would remain during the winter, do what work could be done before the snow came, and then continue the work in the spring.

The land was secured at a small outlay. The canal was surveyed and a little digging was done that fall. When the snow came, Rupert rode twenty-one miles to the county seat, took the teachers' examination, received a certificate, and obtained the Chamogo district school for the winter. It was a new experience for him, and a trying one at first. The big boys came to school to get out of the storm, and incidentally, to learn something of the three R's. They were often wild, but Rupert managed them without doing any "licking," the usual mode of discipline. He now wrote to his sister Nina, and told her that he was located for the winter; that he expected to get back to Willowby, but not for a time.

So the winter months passed. Rupert studied his own lessons when he was not preparing for his day's work. He made frequent visits to the Jansons, though it was a good three miles' drive. He was always received as a friend, and, indeed, was treated as one of the family.

Was it strange that a tie should grow between Rupert Ames and Signe Dahl? Was it anything out of the way that Rupert's trips became more frequent, and that the fair-haired Norwegian looked longingly down the road for the schoolmaster's horse?

Rupert did not try to deceive himself. It had been a year only since his experience with Virginia Wilton. He had thought that he never would get over that, but even now he could look back on it with indifference, yes, even with thankfulness. This love which seemed to be coming to him was different from that first experience. He could not explain this difference, but he knew that it existed. Rupert had no misgivings. Signe did not thrill him, did not hold him spell-bound with her presence. No; it was only a calm, sweet assurance that she was a good girl, that he loved her, and that she thought well of him. Their conversations were mostly on serious, but deeply interesting subjects. Signe, in common with her cousin and Mr. Janson, had religious views of her own, which were peculiar, at least to Rupert. Nothing more than the common doctrines of the Christian denominations had Rupert ever heard. Signe knew her Bible well, and she could find wonderful things within its lids, teachings which were new to Rupert, but which opened to him a future, a bright, glorious future, full of possibilities. Besides, they explained to him many of the mysteries of life and answered many of its hard questions.

Thus one evening — it was Friday, and he lingered longer on that evening—Mr. and Mrs. Janson were visiting neighbors, and Rupert and Signe were alone. They sat by the kitchen stove, and the blazing pine wood made a lamp unnecessary. Signe had received a letter from home which she had translated to Rupert. Her father had long since forgiven her.

The few dollars she sent home now and then multiplied to quite a few *kroner* by the time they reached Norway, and they helped the struggling family. After old country topics had been exhausted, the conversation had drifted to religious themes, and especially to the doctrine expressed in the song "O my Father;" but they now sat silently looking into the fire. Their chairs were not far apart, and it was an easy matter for Rupert to lay his hand over Signe's fingers that rested on the arm of her chair and draw them closely into his big palm.

"Signe," he said, "if we ever lived as intelligent beings in a pre-existent state—and I now can not doubt it,—we two knew each other there. Perhaps we were the closest friends, and I have just been letting my imagination run wild in contemplating the possibilities."

"Let me tell you someting—thing. Did I get tha-at right?"

"You get the th as well as I, and the w's trouble you no more."

"Only sometimes I forget. I was going to say, you remember the first night you came here?"

"I certainly do;" and he pressed her fingers a little closer.

"Well, I seemed to know you from the first. Though you looked bad and like a tramp, I knew you were not, and I felt as if I had known you before."

They were silent again, "reading life's meaning in each other's eyes."

Signe filled the stove from the box beside it.

"You remember that book you gave me to read the other day, Signe?"

"Yes; what do you think of it?"

"I have been thinking considerably about it. It sets forth gospel doctrine altogether different from what I have ever heard; still it agrees perfectly with what Christ and His disciples taught. You know, I have always been taught that man is a kind of passive being, as regards the salvation of his soul; that everything has been done for him; that, in fact, it would be the basest presumption on his part to attempt to do anything for himself; that man is without free agency in the matter; that he is simply as a lump of clay, and with little more intelligence or active powers."

"I know all about such teachings," said Signe, as she went for her Bible. They were drilled into me in the old country."

"Now," continued he, "I see that such doctrines lower man, who is, in fact, a child of God. I cannot perceive that an Allwise Parent would thus take away the agency of His children. We have a motto in school which says: 'Self effort educates,' and I believe that to be the only principle upon which we can safely grow, if we are to become like unto our Eternal Father."

"Yes," answered Signe, "but you must remember one thing, that 'as in Adam all die, even so in Christ shall all be made alive.' The resurrection from the dead comes through Christ without any effort on our part. We were not responsible for

Adam's transgression, therefore we are redeemed from its effects through the atonement of Christ, all mankind are, both good and bad—all will arise and stand before God to be judged by the deeds done in the body."

"Yes; I admit all that; but it is hardly plain to me what we must do to be freed from our individual sins. We are in the midst of sin. We are in a mortal state and partake of our surroundings. Now, there must be a plan by which we may be rid of these imperfections, for if we are ever to live in the presence of God, it seems to me that we must be pure and holy, without sin."

Signe.had her book open. "I will read here an answer to your question," she said. "You remember that on the day of Pentecost when the Holy Spirit was given, Peter preached to a large crowd of people. Many of them believed, and being pricked in their hearts, they said: 'Men and brethren, what shall we do?' You know they are not the only ones who have asked that question."

"No, you are right."

"'And Peter said unto them, Repent, and be baptized every one of you in the name of Jesus Christ for the remission of sins, and ye shall receive the gift of the Holy Ghost.' That's plain enough, isn't it? Words can make it no clearer. When Peter saw that they had faith, he told them to repent, then be baptized for the remission of their sins, then they would get the Holy Ghost."

"And the promise was to them and to their children and to them that were afar off. Signe, is it not to us also?" Rupert asked, eagerly, "why shouldn't it be?"

"The promise is not limited—it is to you and to me. I, Rupert, have obeyed Peter's word, and have received the promise. You may do the same, and the same blessings will follow. The gospel is a law, a natural law, and oh, such a beautiful one!"

"Why haven't I heard this before?" exclaimed he. "Why isn't it written in our books, and taught us in our childhood? Signe, I am a bit bewildered yet."

"Rupert," said she, with a smile that had something of sadness in it, "the world is 'Ever learning but never able to come to the knowledge of the truth.' 'Darkness has covered the earth and gross darkness the people.' 'And as with the people, so with the priest.' 'The earth also is defiled under the inhabitants thereof; because they have transgressed the laws, changed the ordinance, broken .the everlasting covenant.' Is there any wonder that you have not heard these doctrines before? Though you may read about them in the Bible, the world has been without their living presence for many hundreds of years. But a new time has come to the world. The gospel in its fulness and purity has been restored. We read here that John, on the Isle of Patmos, saw that in the latter days an angel would 'fly in the midst of heaven, having the everlasting gospel to preach to them that dwell on the earth.' That angel has come, Rupert, that gospel has been restored; and what I have been telling you are the teachings of that gospel. Man is again endowed with power from on high to preach the gospel and administer its ordinances to those who believe."

Rupert listened with deepest interest. He became as a disciple at her feet. They talked far into the night, and when Mr. and Mrs. Janson came home they found them bending low over the fire reading from the "good old book." Their heads were close together, the dark-brown one and the one of soft, silken tresses.

X.

"I have fought a good fight, I have finished my course, I have kept the faith."—*II Tim. 4:7.*

Rupert was now continually thinking of the great questions of life. Never before had he been so stirred in his feelings; never before had he contemplated life in the light which now came to him. His heart was full of love, gratitude, and praise which swelled within him, and seemed to take possession of his whole being.

The winter passed, and Rupert closed his school. He came to the conclusion that school teaching was not his forte, though the people were satisfied with his work. He longed to be out digging ditches. He liked it far better, and conjectured that in this world his mission was to make the physical deserts to blossom as the rose.

During the summer, Chamogo valley did undergo a change. One side of the valley was brought under irrigation, and a number of farms were sold at a good profit. Mr. Janson did right by Rupert, and together they worked and prospered.

And that which now filled Rupert's cup of happiness was the fact that he had rendered obedience to the gospel of Jesus Christ, and had received the promised gifts and blessings following. The light that leadeth into all truth was his. With Signe and her co-religionists, he could now see eye to eye, all having the same glorious hope for the future.

One more winter passed; and when nature had spread her robe of green over Chamogo valley, preparations were made for the ceremony that would make Rupert and Signe husband and wife. Rupert longed to see Willowby and Dry Bench once more, so it was decided that after they had visited the Temple of God and had been sealed to each other for time and all eternity, they would take a trip to Rupert's old home. They were married in the Temple. Within its sacred walls they experienced more fully than ever before what still sweetness there is in the ministrations of the Spirit of God.

They reached Willowby late in September. He had written Nina when he would be there, and she and her husband were at the station to meet them.

There were tears in their eyes at the meeting.

"Nina, this is my wife," said Rupert. "Signe, my sister, Mrs. Furns."

A number of Rupert's old friends were there who now came forward and welcomed him home.

Then they rode through the valley behind two spirited grays. Nina had not changed much, but she declared that had she met her brother on the street, she would not have known him.

"What has changed you so, brother?" asked she.

"Experience, Nina, experience with the world. I have lived a long time in the two and a half years that I have been away—but never mind that now. Everything looks the same hereabouts. I seem to have been absent but a few days. How strange it is! Signe, there you see Willowby, on that rise; quite a town yet. How's Dry Bench, James?"

"Much the same, Rupe. No improvements since you left."

"And the reservoir?"

"As you left it, though it needs repairing badly."

In the few moments of silence that followed, Rupert contrasted his condition now with what it was when he left the place. What a change! He was wiser if not much older. And then he had a wife—and he looked lovingly at her as he thought of all she had done for him. As they drove into town, friends greeted him and seemed pleased at his return. Married? Yes; that his wife. Not so dashing as Miss Wilton, but far more charming, was the general expression.

That evening there was quite a social gathering at Nina's.

Early next morning, before others of the household were astir, Rupert and Signe went up to Dry Bench. A beautiful morning greeted them. They walked up towards the hill that they might get a good view of the farm, and when they turned, Dry

Bench was before them. The trees had grown, but otherwise it was the same scene that he had looked upon many and many a time. The memory of a particular morning came to him—the morning when Miss Wilton's horse had run away. Miss Wilton had never been heard of since she left Willowby.

"How beautiful!" exclaimed Signe. "Do you know, Rupert, it reminds me of a scene in Norway. I must make a sketch here before we leave."

"Sit down on this rock," said he, "while I tell you something. Here's my overcoat." He made a seat for her and he stood by her side.

"Signe, nearly six years ago, I stood here on this spot. I was the owner of the farm that you see. In fact, I dug this ditch. I set out that orchard, I planned and built the reservoir that has made all this possible; and then I stood here, and in the pride of my heart I said: 'All this is mine. I have done it all.' Now I understand that God put me on trial, lent me some of His riches to try me, and then, seeing that I was not in a condition to stand such favors, took them all from me. Yes, it was a blessing in disguise. Darling, for this knowledge I am indebted to you," and he leaned over and kissed her.

"There you are wrong again," she said; "what about God above?"

"You are right. 'Tis He only who should have our gratitude. You have been but an instrument in His hand. I see it all. O Father, forgive my foolish thoughts." He uncovered his head, as if in prayer.

He sat down with her on the stone. The smoke began to rise from the chimneys of the town below, and soon the Dry Bench farm-houses showed signs of life. He pressed her cheek against his own.

"Sweetheart," said he, " 'When love has blended and molded two beings in an angelic and sacred union, they have found the secret of life; henceforth they are only the two terms of the same destiny, the two wings of one mind. Love and soar.' That is from Victor Hugo; how true it is."

After a time they went down to the old home. A Mr. Temming was living there, as a renter. He was not acquainted with Mr. Ames, and was not disposed to show much courtesy, so they left.

"What do you think of the place?" he asked.

"I like it."

"Could you live there?"

"All my life, I could. Rupert, I see you in every tree, fence, and ditch."

He laughed at that

"I can now buy the place. Shall I?"

"Yes, do."

"You don't object? Would you really like to live there?"

"I think, my dear, that you can do much good here. We ought to live where we can do the most good."

And so it was settled. Next day Rupert inquired after the owner of the farm which once was his, and learned that it was in the hands of a real estate dealer. He made his way to the office and knocked at the door, which was partly open. A man was sitting at a desk, but he evidently did not hear, so Rupert stepped into the room, at the same time giving the door another loud rap. Still the man did not hear.

"Good morning, sir," said Rupert.

The man turned.

"Volmer, Volmer Holm, is it you?"

"Rupert Ames, I'm pleased to see you. When did you come to town? Have a chair."

"Are you in the real estate business?"

"I can't hear very well, and you'll have to speak at close range, Rupe."

So they put their chairs close together, and Rupert repeated his last question.

"Yes, a man must do something; but there's nothing going on now—nothing in our line."

Rupert looked in pity at his friend. Quite shabbily dressed he was, and a careworn expression on his face made him look ten years older. He wore glasses, which he pushed up on his forehead, and then took a good look at Rupert.

"Well, well, Rupe, and where have you been keeping yourself? An' I've had luck, I tell you—you haven't heard, perhaps?"

"No; I haven't. What's it been, Volmer?"

"Was getting fifty dollars a week leading the orchestra at the Grand in Chicago, when I got sick. Don't know what it was, Rupe—the doctors didn't know. Got into my ears, and that knocked me—couldn't tell one note from another; so, of course, that let me out. Hard luck, Rupe, hard luck. Tough world this, Rupe. Why God Almighty crams a fellow's head full of music, and then disables him so's he can't make use of it, I don't know—I don't know."

Rupert sympathized with his friend, and then told him of his errand. A ray of sunshine seemed to enter the musician's life. The property was for sale, yes, and cheap, dirt cheap; so the transaction was partly arranged, and Volmer Holm went home to his wife and four children with quite a happy heart that day.

"It's too bad about Volmer Holm," said Rupert to his sister. "I had not heard of his misfortune. Such a genius in music, too."

"Well, I don't know," answered Nina, "it may be all for the best. Rumor had it that he was fast getting into bad ways in Chicago; and some men are better off by being poor, anyway."

"Yes, that's so," was all he said.

Rupert Ames was again the owner of Dry Bench farm, and the next spring they moved into the old home. Mr. and Mrs. Janson came with them to visit, but their interests in Chamogo would not allow of a protracted stay. Signe was already in love with her new home. With her taste for the artistic, she soon had the place comfortable, and Rupert was never more satisfied than when he came in where his wife's adept fingers had been at work to adorn. It was the dear old home to him with an added beauty, lacking only his mother's presence to make it perfect.

Then they sent for Signe's family. It was hard for the father to make ends meet in his native land, and Rupert needed just such help as Hr. Dahl could give. In due time they arrived, and were installed in a cottage near Rupert's farm.

In peace and prosperity, the days, months, and years went by; and Rupert Ames became a light to the surrounding world, and a teacher of righteousness to his brethren.

It was the sixth year after Rupert's return that the citizens of the Bench decided to enlarge the reservoir in Dry Hollow. Rupert was given the work to supervise, and he entered upon the task with his usual energy.

That morning in September, when he gave his wife the usual departing kiss, the children—four of them, were hanging about his legs and clinging to his coat in great glee.

"Now papa must go," said he, as he tried to shake them off.

"A kiss, another kiss," "A tiss, some more tisses," they shouted.

So he lifted them up, one by one, and kissed them again. Then his arm went around his wife's neck, and he drew her face to his.

"Goodbye, sweetheart," said he, "take care of the children, and don't forget me," and he tried to hum a song as he walked to the gate. Signe stood watching him. The tune which floated back to her was, "O, my Father." Then a peculiar feeling came over her, and she sat down crying, while the children climbed over her with questions and comforting words.

Terrible news from Dry Hollow! A blast, prematurely exploded, had seriously injured some of

the workmen, and Rupert Ames had been killed—
hurled down the ravine and nearly buried under falling rock.

Break the news gently to his wife and children.
Do not let them see that bruised, bleeding form. Spare
them all you can.

Yes; it was all done—all that lay in human power
was done; and hundreds of people to whom Rupert
Ames had opened up new light, and in the providence
of God, had given them a tangible hope of the future,
gathered around his body and mingled their tears
with those of his children's.

Another immortal soul's earthly mission was
ended. Life's school had closed for him. Into another
sphere he had gone. The Great Schoolmaster had
promoted him.

And Mrs. Signe Ames, after it all, simply said:

"God knows best. He has but gone before. He
was my husband for time, he is my husband for eternity. His mission is there, mine is here. In the morrow,
we shall meet again."

XI.

"Go ye into all the world, and preach the gospel to every
creature."—*Mark 16:15.*

Hr. Henrik Bogstad leaned back in his chair
before the fire in great relief. He had just shown
out a young man who was distributing religious
tracts dealing with some "new-fangled religion"
lately imported from America, that land of all new-

fangled things. All the day, Hr. Bogstad had been
adjusting some difficulties among his tenants, and
that evening he was somewhat ill-humored. His treatment of the missionary was, therefore, harsher than
he was wont to treat either strangers or friends.

His conscience smote him a little as he thought
of what the young American had said. He could find
no fault with the religious doctrines advanced, but
why should he be bothered with religion anyway?
He had cares enough; for a great responsibility had
come to him since he had been put in charge of the
estate left by his father's death. Just now was the
season of gaiety in Christiania, and here he was
missing a good many things by his enforced visit to
his country home.

After musing for some time, he got up and went
to the window. Outside, the snow covered everything
—the fields, the roads, the frozen lake and river. The
houses were half hidden, and the pines on the hill
bore up great banks of snow. From the window the
view was beautiful in its solemn whiteness. From the
white level of the distant frozen lake, broken patches
of brown protruded. These were the islands on one
of which Signe Dahl had lived. Henrik wondered
what had become of her, and where in the big America
she had taken up her abode. He had heard that
she was well and happy, but further than that he had
not set himself to learn. Long ago he had put behind
him philosophically his affair with Signe. He had
ceased to think of her as anything more than a sweet,
yet strange girl who could resist such an offer as he
had extended to her.

As Henrik was looking out of the window, he saw the young stranger who had visited him less than an hour ago, returning down the road. Just as he was about to pass, Henrik hailed him and asked him to come in again, meeting him at the door.

"Come in," he said; "I want to talk with you."

The missionary placed his grip on a chair and seated himself on another.

"I was somewhat cross with you when you called," said Henrik. "I don't want you to think that I am rude, especially to strangers."

"I was not the least offended," smiled the other.

"I'm glad to hear it. Now I want you to tell me something about America. I've never been there, though I expect to go some day. I have some friends and a good many relatives over there. From what part do you come?"

"I am from Wyoming."

"That's away out west, isn't it?"

"Yes."

"Two uncles of mine live in Minnesota, but that's a long way from Wyoming. Where are you staying here, for the night?"

"I am a traveling minister of the gospel and I stay wherever there is an opportunity."

"Then you'll stay with me tonight. I am not much on religion, but if you will mix a little information about America with your preaching, I shall be pleased to listen to you."

These conditions were easily agreed to. So, after a good supper, the two young men seated themselves comfortably by the shaded lamp on the library table. The missionary spread out his book of views and explained each of the pictures. He told of the great stretch of arid land in western America, of the ranches, of the high mountains, of the fertile valleys made fruitful by irrigation, and of the wonders of the great Salt Lake.

"This is the Temple."

"Yes; and what is that for?"

The purposes of temples were explained.

"You say you baptize for the dead?" enquired Henrik, "How is that?"

"Well, as I was telling you when I called on you some time ago—"

"Pardon me, but I must confess that I did not pay enough attention to what you said to remember. I was thinking about those quarreling tenants of mine. Tell me again."

The other smiled good-naturedly, and did as he was asked. Henrik listened this time, and was indeed interested, asking a good many questions.

"Now, about the Temple," continued the missionary—"we believe that every soul that has ever lived on the earth, that is living now, or that will ever live must have the privilege of hearing this gospel of Jesus Christ. There is only one name given under heaven by which men may be saved, and every creature must hear that name. Now, the great majority of the human race has never heard the gospel; in fact, will not hear it in this life."

"Where, then, can they hear it?"

"In the great spirit world. Christ, when He was

put to death went and preached to the spirits in prison
—those who were disobedient in the days of Noah
and were destroyed in the flood; and no doubt the
saving power of Christ has been proclaimed in that
spirit world ever since. Among those who hear, many
will believe. They have faith, they repent of their
sins, but they can not be baptized in water for the
remission of their sins."

"No; of course not."

"And yet Christ definitely said that unless a man
is born again of water and of the spirit he cannot
enter into the kingdom of God. What is to be done?"

The listener, leaning over the table, merely shook
his head.

Paul speaks in I Cor. 15:29 of some who were
baptized for the dead—and that is a correct principle. The living may be baptized for the dead, so
that those who have left this world may receive the
gospel in the spirit world and have the birth of the
water done for them vicariously by someone in the
flesh."

"This is strange doctrine."

"Temples are used for these baptisms. The
Latter-day Saints are busy tracing back as far as
possible their lines of ancestry, and then they are
going into their temples — for they have already
four of them — and are doing this work for their
dead. In this way is being fulfilled Malachi's pre-
diction that Elijah the Prophet should come before
the great and dreadful day of the Lord, 'and He shall
turn the heart of the fathers to the children, and

the heart of the children to their fathers,' lest the Lord come and smite the earth with a curse. You will find this in the last chapter of the Old Testament."

The lamp burned late into the night as these two men sat by it talking; and the conversation was not, as one of them had planned, for the most part about the land of America and its material opportunities.

XII.

"Whosoever he be of you that forsaketh not all that he hath, he cannot be my disciple."—*Luke 14:33.*

"I cannot understand him," Frue Bogstad was saying. "His actions are so strange."

"It's simply wicked of him," added Froken Selma Bogstad. "He is bringing the whole family into disrepute."

The mother did not reply, but turned her face thoughtfully away from the angry daughter.

"The boy is completely carried away with this American religion," continued the girl, pacing nervously back and forth in the room. "Pastor Tonset called to see him the other day, and you ought to have heard them! The pastor, as our friend, came to advise him; but do you think Henrik would take any advice? Why, he even argued with the pastor, saying that he could prove the truth of this religion from the Scriptures."

"Has he talked to you about it?"

"Yes; and he wanted me to accompany him to Osterhausgaden where these people hold meetings. I told him definitely and forcibly that I didn't want him to mention religion to me."

"He seems to be in such deep earnest."

"And that's the pity of it. It does no good to talk to him. He takes it for granted that he should be persecuted. I believe he is ready to give up everything for this creed that has him in its grasp."

A violent ringing of the bell brought Selma to the door. It was Henrik, who had forgotten his latch key. He hung up his hat, wiped the perspiration from his face, for it was a warm evening; then he said cheerily:

"Spring is coming; I feel it in the air. I'll be glad to get out to Nordal—there is so much to do this summer—"

"Young man," interrupted the sister, "we have been talking about you."

"About my wickedness, I suppose."

"About your foolishness. It isn't very pleasant for us—what you're doing."

"What am I doing? That which is unkind to you, Mother?" He placed his arms lovingly around her shoulders, but she sat without replying, her face in her handkerchief. He turned to Selma.

"What have I done?" he asked. "Do I drink? Do I gamble? Do I steal? Do I lie? Do I profane? Do I treat any of you unkindly? Am I disrespectful to my mother or my sister?"

"You associate with a people known everywhere as the scum of the earth," snapped the sister, as she stood in front of him. "You are disgracing us — the whole Bogstad family — you — but what's the use of talking to you."

"Not a bit of use that way, dear sister. Suppose you answer some of my questions. You accuse, but never bring proof. You would rather believe uninformed people than me. You accept hearsay, but will not listen to the truth I wish to tell you. I have asked you to point out some of the bad things taught by the Latter-day Saints, but so far you have never tried. I have invited you to go with me—"

"Do you think I would thus disgrace myself to appear in their meetings!"

"You will not even read a simple tract; you close your eyes and ears. You push God from you when you say that He does not reveal Himself any more; and so does Pastor Tonset and all his followers. Because I am willing to receive light, even though it comes from a 'sect everywhere spoken against,' I am a bad man. I tell you, my sister, and also you, my mother, I may be looked upon as a disgrace to the Bogstad family, but the time will come when you and all that family will thank the Lord that one member of the family heard the truth, and had courage enough to accept it!"

Selma walked to the door, and now passed out without replying. Henrik sat down by his mother, and the two continued to converse in low, quiet tones.

The mother's hair was white, the face pinched from much suffering, the hands shrunken. Selma's talk disturbed her, as did that of a score or more of

interested relatives; but when she talked with Henrik
alone she was at peace, and she listened quietly to
what he told her. She was so old and weak and tradi-
tionated in the belief of her fathers that she could
grasp but feebly the principles taught her by Henrik;
but this she knew, that there was something in his
tone and manner of speech that soothed her and
drove away the resentment and hardness of heart left
by the talk of others.

"You know, Mother," Henrik was saying, "this
restored gospel answers so many of life's perplexing
questions. It is broad, full of common sense, and
mercy. Father, as you well know, was not a religious
man. When he died, Pastor Tonset gave it as his
opinion that father was a lost soul—"

"Father was a good man."

"I know he was, Mother; and to say that because
he could not believe in the many inconsistencies
taught as religious truths, he is everlastingly lost,
doesn't appeal to me—never did. Father, as all of us,
will continue to learn in the spirit world to which all
must go; and when the time comes, he will, no doubt,
see the truths of the gospel and accept them. And
here is where the beauty of true religion comes in:
it teaches that there is hope beyond the grave; that
salvation is not limited to this life; that every soul
will have a chance, either here or hereafter. You,
Mother, have worried over Father's condition. Don't
do it any more; he will be all right." He felt like
adding that she had more reason to worry over the
living, but he said no more.

Selma came in with the coffee, and no further

discourse was had on religious topics. Although Henrik had quit using coffee with his meals, he occasionally sipped a little in the company of his mother. This evening he took the proffered cup from his sister, who soon withdrew again, and then Henrik and his mother continued their talk. It was along the lines of the old faith, grounded into them and their forefathers since Christianity had been "reformed" in their country. As a boy, Henrik had not been religious, as that term was understood by his people, but nevertheless he had in him a strain of true devotion which the message of the American missionary had aroused. However, this revival within the young man did not meet with the favor of his friends, and he was looked upon as having come under the influence of some evil, heretical power, much to their regret.

"Marie is here," announced Selma from the door.

Henrik arose. "Where is she? I did not know she was in town."

"She is in the east room."

"Tell her to come in."

"She says she wants to see you alone."

"All right. Good night then, Mother. Pleasant dreams to you."

Henrik found Marie sitting by the open window looking over the tops of the shrubbery in the garden. The light from the setting sun bathed her in its glow, increasing the beauty of an already beautiful face. Henrik stepped up behind the girl and placed his hands under her chin. She did not turn her head.

"This is a surprise," he said, "but I am *so* glad to see you. Did you have a pleasant time at Skarpen?"

There was no reply. The young woman still surveyed the garden and the darkening shadows on the lawn.

"What is the matter, little girl?" he asked. He felt the trembling of her chin as she removed his hands.

"No," she replied, "I did not have a good time."

"I'm sorry. What was wrong?"

"You were not there—you were somewhere else, where your heart is more than with me—you were, no doubt at Osterhausgade." She hardened her tone as she proceeded.

"Oh, I'm not there all the time," he laughed.

"You think more of the people you meet there than you do of me, at any rate."

"What makes you think so?"

"You, and your actions. O, Henrik, could you but hear the talk — I hear it, and people look so strangely at me, and pity me. . . . I can't stand it!" She arose as if to escape him, walked across the room, then sat down by the center table. He closed the window blind, then lighted the gas, and seated himself opposite her 'by the table. There was a pause which she at last broke by saying:

"I hear that you are actually going to join those horrid people—is that true?"

There was another long silence as they looked at each other across the table.

"Yes," he said.

"Next week?"

"That was my intention—yes."

"And we were to be married next month?"

"Yes—"

"Well, I want to tell you, Henrik, that if you join those people the wedding day will have to be postponed."

"For how long?"

"For a long, long time."

"Well—I had thought to be baptized next week; but, of course, I can postpone it."

"For good, Henrik—say for good."

"No; I can't say that; for a little while — to please you, to let you think a little longer on the matter. I want you to choose deliberately, Marie. There need be no undue haste. I don't want you to make up your mind unalterably to reject me because of the step which I am going to take."

"I have already made up my mind."

"Marie!"

"You must choose between me or—"

"Don't say it, don't; you'll be sorry some day, if you do; for the less said, the less there is to retract."

Marie arose. "I'm not going to take anything back," she answered with forceful anger. "I thought you loved me, but—I—have been mistaken. I shall not annoy you longer. Good night."

He arose to follow her. "You need not come with

me," she added. "I shall see Selma, and she will accompany me home—not you."

"Very well, Marie."

She turned at the door. "Will you not promise?"

"Promise what?"

"Not to do as you said—not to disgrace—"

"Marie, where the light shines, I must follow; where the truth beckons, I must go. I—"

With a low cry the girl turned and fled from the room.

XIII.

"The Lord alone did lead him.—*Deut. 32:12.*

One beautiful summer evening, Henrik Bogstad was baptized in the waters of the Christiania fjord. After that, the truths of the gospel appeared clearer than ever, and still whisperings of the Spirit, to which he now had legal right, testified to his spirit that he was in the way of salvation, narrow and straight perhaps, but glowing with a light that comforted and cheered.

He told none of his family or friends of his baptism. They had already rejected him as far as they could, and they asked him no questions. His sister would hardly speak to him, and Marie cut him openly. His many uncles, aunts, and cousins were cold and unfeeling. His mother, though feeble, and sinking slowly, was the only one of his family that he could talk to. She seemed to understand and believe him. He felt that in spirit they were one, and he received great comfort from the thought.

About Midsummer the mother died. Then Henrik spent most of his time at Nordal. There was peace in the solitude of the pine-clad hills, there was comfort in the waving fields of grain and the clear-flowing streams. The lake spread out to his view from his window, and he gazed at its beauty, sometimes his mind wandering from the Dahl home on the island westward to unknown America. And America had a new meaning for him now. Before, it had been simply a new wonder-land, with untold possibilities in a material way; but added to this there was now the fact that in America the Latter-day Zion was to be built; there the people of God were gathering, were building temples, preparatory to the glorious coming of the Lord.

Henrik soon caught the spirit of gathering, but he quenched it as much as possible. His brethren in the gospel advised him to remain where he was and do his full duty to his sister and their interests. This he tried to do. He would not quarrel with Selma, but was exceedingly patient and considerate. He would "talk religion" with any of his friends who expressed a desire to do so, but he would not contend.

Henrik mingled more freely with his tenants at Nordal, and they soon became aware of a change in him. He gave them good treatment. Sometimes, there were Sunday services in the large parlor of the Bogstad residence, and the people were invited to attend. They turned out, it must be admitted, more because of Hr. Bogstad's invitation than because of any enthusiasm on their part.

Henrik, during this period of comparative loneliness, read much. He always carried a book in his
pocket when out among the hills and fields, and many
a moss-covered stone became his reading table. He
had procured a number of English books which he
delighted in, for they brought to him much that had
not yet been printed in his own language.

After the harvesting was over that summer,
Henrik directed his attention to another line of work,
pointed out to him by the New Light. He gathered
the genealogy of his forefathers. His was a large
family, and when he searched the old church records
at Nordal, at Christiania, and at a number of other
places he found that the family was an old and
prominent one, reaching back to the ancient Norsemen. He derived a peculiar satisfaction in this work,
and he extended his researches until he had a large
list of names on his mother's side as well as on his
father's. "Among these there are many noble and
true," thought Henrik. "Many will receive the gospel
in the spirit world, and all will have the opportunity.
I shall have the necessary earthly work done for them.
If my labors for the living will not avail, my dead
ancestors shall have their chance. Who knows but
even now the gospel is being preached to them, and
many of them are looking eagerly for someone to do
their work for them." The thought filled him with
enthusiasm.

The following spring Selma married, which
left Henrik quite alone. He met Marie at the wedding festivities. She was silent and quiet. He made
no strong efforts to win her back to him, so they

drifted apart again. Then Henrik arranged his affairs
so that he could remain away for some months. He
said he was going to America to visit his uncles in
Minnesota,—and yes, very likely he would go farther
west. His friends shook their heads misgivingly, but
he only smiled at their fears.

Henrik sailed from Christiania in company with
a party of his fellow-believers, and in due uneventful
time, landed in the New World. He found America
a wonderfully big and interesting country. He went
directly westward first, crossing the great plains and
rugged mountains to the valleys beyond. Here he
found and visited many of his former friends. He
lived with the Latter-day Saints in their homes, and
learned to know their true character and worth.

Then he saw the temples in which the Saints
were doing a saving work both for the living and the
dead. While in conversation with some of the temple
workers, he told them of what he had in the way of
genealogy, which they commended highly, telling
him that he had an opportunity to do much good for
his family.

"I am glad to hear you say that," replied he,
"for you know, this work for the dead was what first
impressed me in the gospel. It came to me naturally,
it seems, for I had no trouble in accepting it."

Henrik learned much regarding the manner of
procedure in this temple work. He could do the work
for the male members of his family, but a woman
must officiate for the female members. This was the
true order, he found.

"Your sister or your wife or any other near relative would be the person to help you in this," said his informant.

Henrik shook his head. "I am the only member of the family that has received the gospel," he replied.

"Then, of course, any other sister in the faith will do; but the blessings for doing this work belongs to the nearest kin, if they will receive it. Have you no relatives in America?"

"Yes; a lot of them are up in Minnesota, but none that I know are Latter-day Saints—but I'll go and find out," he added as an afterthought.

And that is what Henrik did. Within a month he was on his way. He found his Uncle Ole living not far from St. Paul. He was a prosperous farmer with a family of grown-up sons and daughters who were pleased to see their kinsman from the homeland. All the news from all the family had to be told from both sides. Henrik was shown the big farm with its up-to-date American machinery and methods. He was driven behind blooded horses to the city and there introduced to many people. They knew that Henrik was a person of some importance back in Norway, and they wanted to show him that they also were "somebody." That seemed to be the principle upon which they lived. The father and mother still belonged to the Lutheran church. The three daughters had joined a Methodist congregation because their "set" was there. The two boys attended no church.

Henrik was disappointed. He saw plainly that here was no help for him. All these were entrapped by the world. At first, Henrik said nothing about his own religious faith, but after a time he spoke of the subject to one of his girl cousins. She was not the least interested. He tried another with the same result. Then, one day at the table, he told them all plainly what he believed and what he was called. They were merely surprised. "That's all right," said his cousin Jack who voiced the universal opinion, "we live in a free country, you know, where one's religion isn't called into question."

Henrik's other uncle lived in the city. He was a mechanic, having worked for years in the railroad shops. Some months previous he had been discharged, and since then he had operated a small "tinker" shop of his own. Uncle Jens lived in a small rented house. Uncle Ole's visits to his brother were far between. "Brother Jens is shiftless," Uncle Ole said.

Henrik was, however, made welcome in the humble home, and he soon found the family a most interesting one. His uncle was a religious man, having, as he put it, "got religion" some years ago at a Baptist revival. He had joined that church and was an active member in it. The wife and some of the children were devout believers. They indulged in long family prayers and much scriptural reading. This branch of the Bogstad family called the wealthy farmer and his children a "godless lot."

Uncle Jens' oldest daughter, one about Henrik's own age, did not live at home, therefore he did not see her. He was getting well acquainted with the others, but Rachel he did not know.

"I must meet Rachel, too," he said one day to his uncle. "Where can I' find her?"

"She works in a down-town department store; at night she stays with some friends of hers. The fact is that Rachel is peculiar. She is not one with us. She has been led astray—"

"Oh!" cried Henrik

"She is not a bad girl—no, no; but she has been led away into a false religion, and she will talk and argue with us all, I thought it best that she stay away from our home until she comes to her senses; but—"

"What is this religion that has caused her to err so badly?"

"Why, she calls herself a Latter-day Saint."

"What!"

"Yes; I've tried to reason with the girl, but it's been no use."

"I want to see her—now, today," said Henrik. "Give me her address."

"Shall I go with you?"

"No, I can find her,—you need not bother."

Henrik obtained the proper directions, and set out immediately. Was there then one other of his family that had received the gospel—one that could help him? He boarded a car, getting off at the store. Going to the department in which she worked, he asked the floor-walker where he could find Miss Bogstad. Then he saw her behind a counter, resting for a moment, unoccupied. Though she was an American, Henrik could see the Norwegian traits in his fair cousin. She was of the dark type, with round, rosy lips and cheeks, and heavy, brown hair.

"I am your cousin Henrik from Norway," he said as he shook her hand.

Her smile burst into a soft, merry laugh as she greeted him. "I am glad to see you," she said. "I heard you were here, but thought perhaps I might not get to meet you."

He held her hand a long time, as he looked into the pretty, sweet face. Had he been an American, he would, no doubt, have kissed her then and there; but being a Norwegian, he only looked his wonder and pleasure.

They could not talk much because customers had to be served; but Henrik lingered until closing time, saying he would walk home with her that they might talk. She expressed her pleasure at the proposition; and promptly at the closing gong, she donned her wraps and joined him. The day was warm, and he suggested a walk around by the park, where they might sit down on a bench under the trees.

It was a difficult matter for seriously minded Uncle Jens and his family to laugh, and even a smile was seldom seen on their faces; but here was one who seemed bubbling over with merriment — one whose countenance shone as if from an inner light of happiness.

"Rachel," said Henrik, "your father has told me about you."

"Yes," she replied with sobering face, "they think I am a very bad girl,—but—"

"Look here cousin, don't make any apologies. I know, and understand."

He asked her some questions about herself, all of which she answered frankly. Then he told her about himself, which she first met with an astonished stare. He narrated his experiences in Norway, of his trip westward, and the real purpose of his coming to Minnesota. She heard his story with alternating smiles and tears, as it touched her heart. They sat thus for a long time, oblivious to the singing birds above, of the curious passers-by, or the fast falling night. They walked home in the lighted streets, and it was late when he bade her goodnight at the gate.

The next day Henrik had a talk with Uncle Jens which ended in the uncle's closing with a bang the open Bible on the table out of which they had been reading, and then in uncontrolled rage ordering his nephew out of the house. Henrik tried to make peace with his uncle, but it proved useless, so he took his hat and left.

Henrik met Rachel again that evening, and again they sat on the bench under the trees. Once again they became lost to all outward disturbances in the deep concerns which brooded in their hearts and found utterance in their speech.

"I shall remain here a few days more," said he in conclusion, "because I want to get better acquainted with you; and then we must talk over our plans further. Then I shall go back to Norway. In

a few months I shall come back, and we two shall
go westward where the Temples are, and there begin
the work that is ours—the work that the Lord has called
us to do. What do you say to that?"

"Thank you," she replied simply, and with her
usual smile; "I shall be ready."

XIV.

"Rend your heart and not your garments, and turn unto
the Lord your God: for he is gracious and merciful, slow to
anger, and of great kindness."—*Joel 2:13.*

On Henrik's arrival in Norway, the harvesting
was in full swing, and he busied himself with that.
His friends, some of whom were surprised at his return,
asked him what he had found in America, and he
told them freely. Had he discovered the delusion in
his American religion? No, he replied, his faith had
been made stronger. Selma had relented somewhat,
she making him welcome at her home in Christiania.
Here he also met Marie. Henrik treated her as a
friend with whom he had never had differences.
When she saw him back again, browned and hardy,
but the same gentle Henrik, Marie wondered, and
by that wonder her resentment was modified, and
she listened to his accounts of America and his
relatives in Minnesota with much interest. As he
spoke with an added enthusiasm of his cousin Rachel,
the listeners opened their ears and eyes. He told
them freely of his plans, and what he and Rachel were
going to do.

"Yes," he said, "I can see the hand of the Lord in my finding Rachel."— Marie had her doubts, but she said nothing.—"It is all so wonderful to me, and I am only sorry that you folks can't see it!" But they replied nothing.

Henrik wrote often to Rachel, and the letters which he received in reply he usually handed to Selma, and Marie, if she was present. They pronounced them fine letters. "She must be a jolly girl," they said.

"She is," he affirmed; "the most religious and yet the merriest girl I have ever met. That seems a contradiction, but it isn't." Then he went on explaining, and they could not help listening. Henrik studied the two young women to see what impression he might be making. On Selma there was very little, but he believed Marie was overcoming some of her prejudice. Selma told him that Marie loved him as much as ever, and that if he deserted her, it would break her heart.

"But Selma," he exclaimed, "I have never deserted her. It was she who broke the engagement."

"How could she do otherwise;—but she has been waiting, and will still wait in hope."

"I, too, shall do that," he said.

That fall Henrik again sailed for America. Going westward by way of Minnesota, he called for Rachel and took her with him. In one of the Temple cities they found lodgings with some of his friends, and then they entered upon their work for their ancestors. Henrik had a long list of them, and so they were kept busy nearly all the winter. At the end of three months, Henrik asked Rachel if she was tired and wanted a rest.

"Oh, no," she said; "I believe I can do this work all my life. It isn't always easy, but there is so much joy and peace in it. I believe the angels are with us, and I don't want better company."

And so these two were very much contented. They sent letters home telling of the "glorious" time they were having, and the work they were doing. At the opening of spring, Henrik left Rachel to continue the work, he having to go back to Norway. He asked her if she desired to return to her folks in Minnesota, but she said no, not yet.

The early spring months found Henrik in Christiania. He made a trip to Denmark on genealogical research which proved quite successful. The first of June found him back to Nordal.

Midsummer Night came clear and cool. Henrik was in Christiania, and was to be one of a party to spend the night on the hills above the city. Marie was not with them, and Henrik enquired the reason.

"She is ill," said Selma.

"Ill? Where is she?"

"At home. I think you should go and see her."

"Does she want me?"

"Yes."

Henrik excused himself from the party and went immediately to Marie. He found her on the veranda, reclining on a couch. The lamp-light from an open window fell on a pale face, startling in its changed expression. He silently took her hand, her fingers tightening in his grasp. She looked him steadily in the face, her swimming eyes not wavering. Then Henrik knew that he loved this girl yet. For a long time he had tried to forget her, tried to root out his love for her, tried to think that she was not for him. "I'll not try again," he had thought, "for twice now have I been disappointed;" but now a flood of compassionate love engulfed him, and he, too, clung to the fingers in his grasp.

"I am sorry to see you like this," he said, "what is the matter?"

"I don't know."

"Doesn't the doctor know?"

She shook her head with a faint smile. "Sit down, Henrik, I want to talk to you," she said.

He took the low chair by her side. The mother looked at them from the doorway, but did not come out.

"I want you to forgive me," she said.

"That has been done long ago."

"Thank you — now listen. I have been wrong, wickedly wrong, it seems to me—listen! I have not been honest, neither with you, nor myself, nor with the Lord—which is the worst of all. I understood much that you taught me of the restored gospel—It seemed so easy to my understanding; but my pride was in the way, and I would not accept the light. I pushed it away. I kept saying to myself, 'It isn't true,' when I knew all the time that it was. That's the sin I have committed."

"My dear—"

"You remember that book you asked me to read?

Well, I read it through, though I led you to believe
that I did not. It is a beautiful book, and true, every
word.   *   *   * Perhaps you will not believe me
when I tell you that I have been a number of times
to your meetings in Osterhausgade. Once when you
were there—I thought you would see me," she smiled.
"And I could find no faults, though at first I went
looking for them * * * Now, I've told you. You have
forgiven me, you say; but will the Lord?"

"Yes; the Lord is good."

"When I get better—if I do—I am going to join the
Church as you have done. That is the right thing to
do, isn't it?"

"Yes."

"And then, may I go to where you and your
cousin Rachel are working for the dead? When—
when are you to be married?"

"Married? To whom?"

"Why, to your cousin Rachel. Are you not going
to marry her?"

"Certainly not—never thought of it for a moment."

"Oh, dear, I must have made another mistake.
Forgive me." She lay back on her cushions.

"Marie, when I get married, it's you I want for
my wife. I have told you that before, and I haven't
changed my mind. You shall be mine, if you will
come back to the sweet days of long ago. Will you?"

He leaned over the couch, and she drew his face
to hers. "Yes," she whispered.

At the end of an hour's conversation wherein
much had been said, Marie asked: "May I go with

you to the temple and there help you in the work you are doing? I believe I could help a little."

It was at that moment that the curtain lifted from eyes of the mortal, and Henrik saw for an instant into the pre-existent world. A group of spiritual beings was eagerly engaged in conversation, and from out that group he heard the voice of one answering Marie's question.

"Yes; I think so; but we shall see."

XV.

"A friend of mine in his journey is come to me."—Luke 11:6.

The next time Henrik went to the valleys of the mountains in western America, Marie accompanied him. They were married in the Temple, made man and wife for time and eternity by the authority of the Priesthood. That event was among their supremely happy ones. Rachel witnessed the ceremony, and the smile on her face was sweeter than ever.

After that, Marie helped in the temple work as she had desired. The three then labored together until Henrik's list of names was nearly exhausted. After a very pleasant visit among friends, Henrik and Marie went back to Norway and to Nordal. They made a new home from the ancient one on the hillside by the forest, and for them the years went by in peace and plenty. Sons and daughters came to them, to whom they taught the gospel. In time many of his kin also believed the truth and accepted it, and thus the seed that was sown in humility, and at first brought but small returns, gave promise of a bounteous harvest.

Once every four or five years, Henrik and Marie visited the Saints in the West, and spent some time in the temple. These were happy times for Rachel, who continued to live alone, not making many intimate acquaintances. Henrik was glad to provide for her simple necessities, so that she could continue her life's work in behalf of the dead.

Rachel did not marry. Once in Minnesota, a young man had made love to her, but she could not return that love, so she was in duty bound not to encourage him. Rachel was hard to get acquainted with, a number of young men had said. She was always happy and smiling, and yet a closer knowledge of her character disclosed a serious strain that puzzled her admirers—for Rachel had admirers. A number of times good men had been about to make love to her in earnest, but each time some strange feeling had checked them. The young woman was "willing" enough but what could she do? There was without doubt a "man" for her, but she could not go in search of him. As the years went by, and with them her youth and somewhat of her beauty, she was often sad, and sometimes heart-hungry; and at such times she found no peace until she had poured out her heart to her heavenly Father, and said, "Thy will be done—but make me satisfied."

After an absence of three years Rachel visited her home in Minnesota. She was received kindly, the parents being no doubt grateful that she had escaped alive from the clutches of those "terrible people" whom she had been among. She could still smile and be happy, be more patient than ever, taking in good part the ridicule and sometimes the abuse directed toward her. She talked on the gospel with those who would listen, and after a time she found that she was making a little headway. Her father, at the first, told her emphatically that she was not to "preach her religion" in his house; but he would sometimes forget himself and ask her a question, which in being answered would lead to a gospel discourse. Then, awakening to what was going on, he would say, "That will do. I thought I told you that we wanted none of your preaching," at which Rachel would smilingly look around to the others who were also smiling at the father's inconsistencies.

During this visit the good seed was planted, from which in due time the Lord gave an abundant harvest from among the Bogstad family and its many ramifications.

One day in the temple Rachel met Signe Dahl Ames. It was Rachel's custom to keep a lookout for sisters who were new to the work that she might assist them. Signe had not been in the Temple since the day she was married, and now she had come to do some work for her family. Rachel met her in the outer room with a pleasant greeting.

"I am Sister Bogstad," she said; "and what is your name?"

"Bogstad, did you say—why—why, my name is Ames."

"Yes, Bogstad," replied Rachel, noticing the sister's surprise. "We haven't met before, have we?"

"No; I think not. The name is not common and I used to know a gentleman by that name—that's all."

"You're a Norwegian," said Rachel.

"Yes."

"So am I; though I was born in this country, it may be possible that I belong to the family which you know."

"I used to know Henrik Bogstad of Nordal, Norway."

"That's my cousin. We have been doing work here in the temple."

Signe was greatly surprised, and Rachel led her to a corner where they talked freely for some time. During the day they found occasion to continue their conversation, and that evening Signe went home with her new-found friend.

This was the beginning of a beautiful friendship. Rachel knew enough of Henrik's little romance with Signe to make the acqaintanceship unusually interesting; besides, there came to be a strong affinity between the two. Rachel accompanied her friend to Dry Bench, and there soon became "Aunt Rachel" to Signe's four beautiful children. Then she wrote to Henrik, telling him of her wonderful "find." He replied that at their next visit to America, they would surely give Dry Bench a call.

Henrik, Marie, and two of the older children came that fall when the peaches were ripe and the alfalfa fields were being cut. And such delicious peaches, and such stacks of fragrant hay they found! Amid the beautiful setting of the harvest time, their several stories were told, in wonder at the diverging and the meeting of the great streams of Life. The Bogstad children practiced their book-learned English, while the Ames children were willing teachers. The boys bathed in the irrigation canal, rode on the loads of hay, and gorged themselves with peaches. The girls played house under the trees. And were it part of this story, it might be here told how that, later, Arnt Bogstad and Margaret Ames loved and mated—but it is not.

Henrik and Marie lived happily together for twelve years, and then Marie was called into the spirit world. Henrik was left with five children, the youngest but a few months old. With ample means, he could obtain plenty of household help, but money could not buy a mother for his children. A number of years went by, bringing to Henrik new and varied experiences. Then on one of his visits to the West he found another helpmate for himself and children— a kind-hearted, sweet-souled young woman, born of Danish parents, and reared among the Saints in the valleys of the mountains. Then the westward call became so strong that Henrik disposed of most of his interests in Norway and moved with his family to America, taking up his abode in a town not far from Dry Bench. Here they enjoyed the association of the

Saints, and his children had the advantage of companionship of children of the faith.

Time, and the world with it, sped on. Peace and prosperity came to the people of this story. As years were added to years, their good works increased, until the Lord said to each of them, Enough. Then in their own time and place, they passed into the Paradise of God.

I

"They shall be gathered together as prisoners are gathered in the pit, and shall be shut up in prison, and after many days shall they be visited."—*Isaiah 24:22*

The Lord God created all things "spiritually before they were naturally upon the earth." He created "every plant of the field before it was in the earth, every herb of the field before it grew." Before this "natural" creation "there was not yet flesh upon the earth, neither in the water, neither in the air; . . . . . but spiritually were they created and made according" to the word of God. In this second or "natural" creation all things were clothed upon by earthly element, or in other words, the spiritual was materialized so that it became discernible to the natural senses. The spiritual and the natural are, therefore, but different states of the same forms of life. In the natural world there are men, women, beasts of the field, fowls of the air, and vegetation in boundless and varied forms. These exist before the natural is added upon them; they exist after the natural is laid down by the death of the body.

In like manner we find in the spirit world men, women, beasts of the field, fowls of the air, and vegetation in boundless and varied forms. These things are as natural there as they are in earth-life. They appeal to spirit nature the same as the "natural" prototype appeals to the mortal senses; and this is why we may speak of our earth-known friends who are in the spirit world and of their surroundings in the manner of mortality.

And what a big world it is! Here are nations, tribes, races, and families much larger than in earth-life, and just as varied in all that made them different in mortality. Here, as in all of God's creations, like assemble, dislike keep apart; "for intelligence cleaveth unto intelligence; wisdom receiveth wisdom; truth embraceth truth; virtue loveth virtue; light cleaveth unto light; mercy hath compassion on mercy, and claimeth her own." The righteous in Paradise have no desire to mingle with the wicked in the regions of darkness; therefore they go there only as they may be called to perform some duty.

To the industrious there can be no true pleasure or rest in idleness; therefore, Paradise furnishes employment to all its inhabitants. A world of knowledge is open to them into which they may extend their researches. Thus they may continue in the ever-widening field of learning, finding enough to occupy their time and talents.

An arrival in the spirit world brings with him just what he is when he leaves mortality. The separation of the spiritual part of the soul from the earthly body does not essentially change that spirit. A person takes with him the sum total of the character he has formed up to that time. Mortal death does not make a person better or worse; it simply adds to him one more experience which, no doubt, has a teachable influence on him. At death, no person is perfect, even though he is a Saint, and passes into the Paradise of God. There he must continue the process of eliminating the weaknesses which he did not wholly overcome in earth-life. Death will not destroy the tendency to tell untruths, or change the ungovernable temper to one which is under perfect control. Such transformations are not of instant attainment, but are the result of long, patient endeavor.

As there are gradations of righteousness and intelligences in the spirit world, there must be a vast field of usefulness for preaching the gospel, training the ignorant, and helping the weak. As in the world of mortality, this work is carried on by those who have accepted the gospel and who have conformed their lives to its principles; so in the spirit world, the righteous find pleasant and profitable employment in working for the salvation of souls.

And as they work they must needs talk of the glories of the great plan of salvation, made perfect through the atonement of the Lord Jesus. That which they look forward to most keenly, that about which they talk and sing most fervently is the time when they also shall follow their Savior through the door of the resurrection which He has opened for them,—when their souls shall be perfectly redeemed, and they shall be clothed upon with a body of the heavenly order, a tabernacle incorruptible and immortal with which to go on into the celestial world.

Though the future is most glorious to these people, the past is also bright. The hopes of the future are well grounded on the facts of the past. An ever-present theme is that of Christ's first visit to the spirit world, when, having died on the cross, He brought life and light and immortality to the world of spirits, entering even into the prison house where the disobedient had lain for a long time, and preached the gospel to them.

And among these who gloried both in the past and in the future were Rupert and Henrik. Often they conversed on themes near to their hearts:

"It must have been a place of darkness, of sad despairing hearts, that prison house, before Christ's visit to it," said Rupert. "There, as in a pit, dwelt those who in earth-life had rejected the truth, and who, sinking low in the vices of the world, permitted themselves to be led captive by the power of the evil one. Noah in his day preached to them, but they laughed him to scorn and continued in their evil ways. Others of the prophets in their generations had warned them, but without avail; so here were found Satan's harvest from the fruitful fields of the earth."

"I can well imagine that long, long, night of darkness," added Henrik. "No ray of hope pierced the gloom of their abode. The prison walls loomed around and above them, shutting out any glimpse of heaven. These had rejected the truth, which alone can make men free. They themselves had

shut out the light when it would have shone in upon
their vision. They had chosen the evil, and the evil
was claiming its own. Outside the prison were their
fellows who had chosen to do the right, basking in
the light of a clear conscience, enjoying the approval
of the Lord. These faithful ones were going on to
eternal perfection. How long would it take the
prisoners, if they ever were released, to overtake
those ahead? Between these was a great gulf fixed,
which, in the ordinary order of things, could never be
lessened or bridged."

"But at last the time of mercy and deliverance
came. I remember how the events of the time have
been described to me. Just before the coming of the
Lord, a peculiar, indescribable tremor ran through
this spirit world as if one pulse beat through the
universe and that pulse had been disturbed. The
spirits in prison looked in awe at one another, many
crouching in terror, fearful that the day of judgment
had come. The vast multitude of the ignorant wondered what the 'peculiar feeling' could mean. The
righteous, who had been looking wistfully for some
manifestation of the coming of the Lord, whispered
to each other, 'The Lord is dying for the sins of the
world!'

"Yes; the prophets of every dispensation had
labored faithfully to prepare the world of spirits
among whom they lived for the coming of the Lord
and Savior. There were Adam, Noah, Abraham,
with those who followed them; there were Lehi,
Nephi, Mosiah, and the others of their race; there
were the prophets who had lived among the lost

Ten tribes; these had all been valiant in earth-life, and were faithful yet in the spirit world. The burden of their message in mortality had been the coming of Christ the Redeemer, and now they still looked forward with the eye of faith to Him who should die for the sins of the world, and who should deliver them from the bondage of the grave. They understood that the body of flesh which had been given them in mortality was necessary for their full salvation. Christ would bring to pass the resurrection, so that bodies would be restored to them, not corruptible as before, but perfected, immortal and glorious, a fit tabernacle for the immortal spirit with which to go on into the eternal mansions of the Father."

"But oh, that time, brother, when the Son of God was dying on the cross! While the earth was shrouded in darkness, and the bulk of it trembled in sympathy with the death throes of its Maker, the spirit world also received the imprint of the terrible event on Calvary as for a moment the whole spiritual creation lay in tense expectancy. The usual occupations were suspended. Speech became low and constrained. Songs ended abruptly, and laughter ceased. There were no audible sobs, neither sighing. Bird and beast were stilled, as if the end had come, and nothing more mattered. Then, in a little while, the tenseness relaxed, and everything went on as before, though much subdued. The righteous in the Paradise of God quietly gathered themselves together in their usual places of worship. They clasped each other's hands, and looked with trembling gladness into each other's faces. There was no fear here: they were ready."

"And then His actual coming! That which had been fore-ordained from before the foundation of the world was about to be fulfilled; that which had been the theme of the prophets from the beginning was at the door; that which the seers of all times and nations had beheld in vision was now to be realized; that about which poets had sung; that for which every pure heart had yearned; that for which the ages had waited, was now here! A feeling of sweet peace filled the righteous, which expressed itself in songs of praise and gladness. Thus they watched and waited."

"Then Jesus stood in their midst, and they beheld the glorious presence of their Lord. Then there came to their hearts a small, sweet, penetrating voice, testifying that this was Jesus Christ the Son of God who had glorified the name of the Father; who was the life and the light of the world; who had drunk of the bitter cup which the Father had given him; and had glorified the Father in taking upon Himself the sins of the world, in which He had suffered the will of the Father in all things from the beginning. The multitude fell down at his feet and worshiped."

"I have been told that as Jesus entered the prison of the condemned in the spirit world, a murmur of greeting welcomed Him. It was timid and faint at first, but it increased in volume and force until it became a shout.

" 'Lift up your heads, O ye gates, and be ye lifted up, ye everlasting doors.' "

" 'Hail, hail, to the Lord.' "

" 'And the King of Glory shall come in.' "

" 'Who is the King of Glory?' "

" 'The Lord, strong and mighty.' "

" 'The Lord, will not cast off forever; but though He cause grief, yet will He have compassion, according to the multitude of His mercies.' "

" 'I will not contend forever, neither will I be always wroth.' "

" 'Come and let us return unto the Lord: for He hath torn and He will heal; He hath smitten, and He will bind us up.' "

" 'I will heal their back slidings, I will love them freely; for mine anger is turned away.' "

" 'Who is a God like unto Thee, that pardoneth iniquity. He retaineth not His anger forever, because He delighteth in mercy.' "

" 'Say to the prisoners, Go forth; to them that are in darkness, show yourselves. I am He that liveth and was dead; and behold I am alive forevermore, anew: and I have the keys of hell and death.' "

"And thus the gates were lifted, and the King of Glory entered. And what a radiance shone in the gloom! The shades of darkness fled, the chains of error dropped asunder, the overburdened heart found glad relief, for the Lord brought the tidings of great joy to the spirits in prison, offering them pardon and peace in exchange for their broken hearts."

"Then they sang:

' "Hark, ten thousand thousand voices
 Sing a song of Jubilee!
A world, once captive, now rejoices,
 Freed from long captivity.
Hail, Emanuel! Great Deliverer!
 Hail, our Savior, praise to thee!
Now the theme, in pealing thunders,
 Through the universe is rung;
Now in gentle tones, the wonders
 Of redeeming grace is sung." '

"For three days, as counted by earth-time, the Redeemer ministered in this spirit world, preaching the gospel, giving instructions, and making plain the way of His servants to follow. Joy and gladness filled many hearts. Then, when the time had fully come, the great Captain of Salvation led the way against the enemy of men's souls. He laid low the Monster that had for ages kept grim watch at the Gates of Death. He broke through the grave to the regions of life and light and immortality. The Hope of Ages thus went forth conquering; and those who followed Him through the resurrection from the dead sang:

" 'Death is swallowed up in victory! O, death, where is thy sting? O grave, where is thy victory?' "

II.

"Whatsoever a man soweth, that shall he also reap. For he that soweth to his flesh shall of the flesh reap corruption; but he that soweth to the Spirit shall of the Spirit reap life everlasting."—*Gal. 6:7, 8.*

In the spirit world are Rupert, Signe, Henrik,

Marie, Rachel and all our friends in their time and place. These are employed in joyous activity, as they see their field of usefulness continually widen. Rupert had done 'a great work before the others had come. He had preached the gospel to many people, mostly his ancestors, among whom there had been at the time of his arrival among them an awakening and a desire for the truth. He had traced his family back to those who on earth had been known as the Pilgrim Fathers, thence through many generations to the Norsemen of northern Europe. His wife's family he had also searched out, and he had discovered, greatly to his delight, that her family and his met in a sturdy, somewhat fierce, Viking chief. Rupert had sought him out, and had told him of Christ and His gospel—and the Viking had been willing to be taught. When Signe had come, Rupert had brought her to visit her many-times-great-grandmother, who was a beautiful flaxen-haired, blue-eyed woman, whom Signe herself somewhat resembled.

Then when Rupert met and became acquainted with Henrik, Marie, and Rachel, he told them of what he had done, and how that their vicarious work for the dead had fitted so nicely in with his preaching, in that many of those for whom they had been baptized were those whom he had converted. "We have been working in harmony and in conjunction," exclaimed Rupert, "and God's providence is even now clearly justified." What joy was there when Henrik and his friends met those for whom they had performed the necessary earthly rites!

Many of these had long ago believed the gospel, and their hearts had been turned to their children — their descendants living on the earth — that they would remember their fathers who had gone before; and these were overjoyed when they met their "saviors," as they called them. Then, there were others who had not accepted the work done for them, and these were, naturally, not so enthusiastic in their greetings. Others there were who were yet in ignorance of Christ, of His plan of salvation, and the work that had been done for them. These would have to be taught and given a chance to accept or reject what had been done.

"You enjoy a happiness that does not come to me," said a brother to Henrik, "in that you receive the love and joyous greetings of those for whom you did work in mortality."

"Had you no opportunity to do such work?" asked Henrik.

"Yes; but I had no names of ancestry, and the truth is, I did not try to get any."

"You did not do all in your power?"

"No; I was careless in the matter."

"If you had only tried, the way would have been opened. That is a true principle. We do not know what regions of usefulness lie before us if we do no exploring."

Signe and Rachel were closely associated, and they performed missions together to their less enlightened sisters whose condition was not so favorable. These were of the frivolous and foolish women who had been taken captive by earthly things. All

their treasures had been of earth, so on earth they
had to be left, for none could be taken into the spirit
world; these, therefore, were poor indeed. They had
nothing with which to occupy themselves: in earth-
life, wealth, fashion, the gratification of depraved
appetites and passions, and the pampering of worldly
vanities had been their chief concern; and now that
earthly things were no more, these women were as
if lost in a strange world, having no sure footing,
groping about in semi-darkness, hungering and
thirsting, but finding no means by which they might
be satisfied. They laughed and appeared to make
merry because it was their nature so to do, but their
laugh was empty, and their merriment rang hollow
and untrue.

"I am more than ever thankful," said Signe to
Rachel when they had labored long with a group of
frivolous women, "that the gospel reached us in earth-
life."

"And that we accepted it," added Rachel.

"Yes; many of these sisters of ours are not evil;
they are just weak,—empty of good. Their earthly
training was at fault. And then some of them have
told me that they were very much surprised to find
that death had not worked a transformation in them:
they have still the same feelings, desires and thoughts
as before."

"Some foolish things were taught in earth-life,"
said Rachel, "one of them being deathbed repentance.
Common sense, if not reason, ought to have told us
that a change of heart coming when a person is in
full possession of his faculties is far better than the

confessions made in fear of death. Repentance should
have come further back, for the sooner we turn about
on the right way, the further we get on the road to
perfection."

Rachel finished her little speech with a smile—
the simple sweet smile, fixed into her nature for all
time. A strange sister came up to her, who was greeted
pleasantly.

"I want to know more of you two," she said.
"There is something about you different from me or
my mates. When you mix with us and talk with us,
I can feel it, but I don't know what it is. You appear
to me to be, lilies-of-the-valley among weeds—yes,
that's it."

"And isn't a weed just a useful plant grown
wild?" asked Signe. "All it needs is careful cultivation. Come with us as we walk along. We shall be
pleased to talk with you. We are not very wise, but
we may always ask the brethren who are wiser, for
more light."

And so these three went slowly along the beautiful paths of spirit-land, conversing as they went.
The hazel eyes of the brown-haired stranger opened
in wide astonishment at what her sisters told her.
Sometimes she asked questions, sometimes she shook
her head in disbelief. She had been a "worldly"
woman, she told them, never thinking that there
would be any life other than the one she was living
while on the earth; and so she had shaped her daily
conduct by that narrow standard. Her earth-life
had ended sadly, and existence had been bitter ever
since, "Restless and hopeless, I have wandered for

a long time," she said. "I have seen you two a number of times and have heard you talk to the women.
Your words seemed to bring to me a glimpse of
something better, but I never had the courage to speak
to you until now."

Signe put her arms around her, drew her close,
and kissed her cheek. "Let us do you all the good
we can," she said. "We are going now to attend
a meeting where my husband is to speak. Come with
us."

Rachel linked her arm into that of the stranger's
who willingly accompanied them. "Is your husband
also a preacher?" she asked of Rachel.

"I have no husband," was the reply. "I did not—
I mean, he did not find me, has not found me yet."
Rachel was somewhat confused but she smiled as ever.

"She means," explained Signe, "that she did not
marry while in earth-life, for the very good reason
that she had no chance—"

"None such that I could accept," added Rachel.
Then as the newly-found friend looked at her inquir-
ingly, she continued:

"I have always believed, and I believe now, that
I have a mate somewhere, but he has not yet been
revealed. Frequently I asked the Lord about it in
earth-life, and the answer by the spirit always was
'Wait, patiently wait'; so I am still waiting."

"And you still have faith," asked the stranger,
"that the God of heaven will answer your prayers
and bring about all things for the best?"

"Why, certainly."

"I wish I could believe that. Had I in earth life had some such belief to anchor to, perhaps I would not have made so many mistakes. I married twice, and they were both mistakes. The one chance I had of getting a man—I mean, one who does not belie the word—I threw away, because he was poor in worldly goods; but I suffered through my foolish errors . . . . . I have heard of people praying about many things, but never have I heard of the Lord being asked about love affairs."

"That may be true," said Signe; "and it shows how foolish we were. Why should people importune the Lord about small trials and petty ailments, and at the same time neglect to ask His guidance on matters of love and marriage which make or mar one's life?"

There seemed to be no immediate answer to this query, so the three passed along in silence. Presently the newcomer spoke again:

"I am getting more light and hope since I associate with you two. I believe my faith is being kindled, and O, it feels so good to get a little firm footing."

"Yes, dear sister," said Rachel. "The tangled threads of earth-life are not all straightened out yet. It will take time, and we must have patience."

Arriving at the place of meeting, the three women took positions near the platform upon which the speakers sat. Rupert was the principal speaker. He began by telling his listeners something about his experiences in earth-life. He spoke of his boyhood days, of the trials and difficulties he had en-

countered, and how near he had come to being lost
to all good. Then he told how the Lord had rescued
him, and brought him to a knowledge of the gospel
of salvation. "And the Lord's chief instrument in
this work of rescue," the speaker said, "was a beautiful, good woman, who became my wife. O, you
women, what power you have for good or evil! See
to it that you use your powers for the purpose of
good."

Rachel smiled at Signe while they listened, for
Rupert's and Signe's story was quite familiar to her.
All the time Rupert had been speaking, the woman
who had come with them sat as if spellbound, her
big eyes fixed on the speaker. When Rupert closed,
Signe said to her friend:

"That is my husband. Let us go up to him; he
will be glad to meet you."

But the woman drew back as if afraid. "I can't,"
she whispered. "Forgive me, but I must go"—and
with a faint cry she retreated and disappeared in
the crowd, the two women looking after in wonder
and astonishment.

Just then Rupert stepped up to them. Seeing their
wonder, he asked the reason. Signe explained.

"I think I can guess who it was," said Rupert.
"Well, well," he murmured as if to himself, "I had
nearly forgotten her."

"Yes, I believe it was she," added Signe.

"Was who?" inquired Rachel.

But Rupert stopped any reply that his wife might
wish to make by interrupting with:

"I saw an impressive sight not long ago—Come,

let us be getting on our way home, and I shall tell it
to you."

They were willing to listen as they journeyed.
"We were out," began Rupert —"a brother and I —
getting some information needed in one of the temples on earth for a brother who had gone as far as
he could with his genealogy. As we were talking to
a group of sisters a man rushed in upon us. With
quick, eager words he asked us if we had seen someone whom he named and described. At the sight of
him, one of the women shrunk back as if to hide in
the crowd, but he saw her, and exclaimed:

"'Is that you? Yes — Oh, have I found you at
last!'"

"The sister put forth her hand as if to ward him
off, as he pressed through the crowd to her. 'How
did you get here?' she asked. 'Keep away—you are
unclean—keep away.'

"He paused in some astonishment at this reception. Then he pleaded with her to let him accompany her; but she retreated from him crying, 'You
are unclean; do not touch me.'

"'Yes,' he acknowledged, 'I suppose I have been
a sinner; but listen to my justification: I sinned to
drown my sorrow when you died. I, also, wanted to
die. My heart was broken—I could not stand it—it
was because I loved you so—'

"'No; you did not love me. Love is pure —
made purer by sorrow. Had you truly loved, you
would not have sinned so grievously. Your sorrow
needed to be repented of. Sorrow cannot be drowned

in sin—no, no; go away. Please go; you frighten
me.

"The man stood rigid for some time, and the
expression on his face was something terrible to see.
The cold, clear truth had for the first time burst
upon him to his convincing. He had a 'bright recollection of all his guilt,' and his torment was 'as a lake
of fire and brimstone.' The woman, recovering somewhat from her fright, stood before him with innocent,
clear-shining eyes, with half pity and half fear showing in her beautiful countenance – for the woman
was beautiful. The man stood for a moment, which
seemed a long time to all who witnessed the scene,
then his head dropped, his form seemed to shrivel
up as he slouched out of our company and disappeared
from sight."

There was silence. Then Rupert added, "And yet
some people tried to make us believe that there is
no hell."

Rachel, even, forgot to ask further questions
regarding the identity of the woman with hazel eyes
and auburn hair, for just then Henrik and Marie
appeared. With them was another woman, and the
three were so preoccupied that they were oblivious
to all others.

"You are too late for the meeting," said Rupert.

"I did intend to get there in time," replied Henrik,
"but don't you see who is here?"

Rupert did not recognize the woman who stood
by Marie with arms about each other, but Signe cried
in joyous greeting, "Clara, Clara, is that you?"

"This is Clara," said Marie to Rupert, "she who

came to Henrik after I left him,—who helped him
so much, and who was so good to my children. She
has just come, and has brought us much good news
from them. I am so glad." Marie's arm drew tight
around the newcomer as she kissed her cheek.

"I, also, am glad to welcome you," said Rupert.
"Brother Henrik," he added, "your excuse from non-
attendance at our meeting is accepted."

III.

"The Lord . . . will fulfill the desire of them that fear him;
he will also hear their cry."—*Psalms 156:19.*

Rachel found continual delight in all the wonders of spirit-land. Her circle of acquaintances enlarged rapidly, as those for whom she had done temple
work were glad to know her, and to know her was
to love her. These brought her in touch with many
others; thus her sphere of usefulness extended until
she, too, could say that she was busier than ever in
joy-giving activities.

Sometimes Rachel went on what she called "excursions of exploration." Usually she went alone,
for the habit of doing things of herself still clung
to her. Frequently, in the throngs of people with
whom she mingled, she was accosted by someone
who recognized her. Rachel did not remember faces
easily, but (she was on one of her excursions) she
knew this woman who touched her on the arm, and
said:

"You are Sister Rachel, are you not?"

"Yes; and you—yes, I know you. I am glad to meet you. How are you? Has the Lord shown you, —has He satisfied you? You see I remember you well."

The woman showed her gladness at Rachel's recognition. "The Lord has shown me abundantly and graciously," she replied; "but come with me away from the crowd. I shall be pleased to tell you all about it." Rachel accompanied the woman, who led her out into some quieter streets, thence to a beautiful home under tall trees. Flowers bloomed and birds sang in the garden. The two women seated themselves by a playing fountain.

"I am glad you have not forgotten me. My name you may not remember—it is Sister Rose."

"Your face, dear sister, your beautiful face marked with that deep sorrow, no one could forget;" said Rachel, "but now the sorrow is gone, I see, and the beauty remains."

Sister Rose took the other's hand caressingly. "That day in the temple," she said, "I came there as a place of last resort. I was suffering, and had tried everything that I could think of to ease my troubled soul. I had prayed to God to give me some manifestation regarding my boy. I came to the temple to get a great favor, and I obtained a bless-ing. Instead of receiving some miraculous mani-festation, you came to me and led me gently to a seat by ourselves. And there you talked to me. It was not so much what you said, but the spirit by which you said it that soothed and quieted and rested me. You repeated to me some verses, do you remember? I had you write them out, and I committed them to memory."

"Do you remember them yet?"

"Listen:

"Thou knowest, O my Father! Why should I
  Weary high heaven with restless prayers and tears!
Thou knowest all! My heart's unuttered cry
  Hath soared beyond the stars and reached Thine ears.

Thou knowest—ah, Thou knowest! Then what need,
  Oh, loving God, to tell Thee o'er and o'er.
And with persistent iteration plead
  As one who crieth at some closed door."

"That day I went away comforted and strengthened. Do you recollect?"

"Yes; but what was your trouble? I do not remember that.

"My son, my only child, was taken so cruelly from me. He was the hope of my life, and when he answered the call to go on a mission to the islands of the sea, I let him go gladly, because it was on the Lord's business. Then some months later the news came that he had died. I was crazed with grief. I could not understand why the Lord would permit such a thing to take place. Was my boy not in His service? Why did not the Lord take care of His own?"

"And so you suffered, both because of your loss and because of your thoughts," said Rachel. "Poor sister,—but now?"

"He is with me now, and it has all been explained.

We live in this house. Do you care to hear the story?"

"If you desire to tell it, yes."

"You seem so near and dear to me that I may tell it to you. My boy, while on his mission, was tempted. He has told me all about it — he was tempted sorely. He was in great danger, and so the Lord, to prevent him from falling into the mire of sin, permitted him to be taken away. They brought his lifeless body home to me, but his spirit went back to its Maker pure and unspotted from the sins of the world,—and thus I found him here, a big, fine-looking man as he was. You ought to see him."

"Mother," someone called from the direction of the house.

"That is he now," said the mother, rising.

"Mother, where are you? Oh!" the son exclaimed as he caught sight of the two women. He came up to them and rested his arm tenderly on his mother's shoulder. He was big and handsome, and Rachel's eyes dropped before his curious gaze.

"David, this is Sister Rachel, whom I first met in earth-life in the temple. I think I have told you about her and what a comfort she was to me."

"I am very glad to know you," said he, as he clasped Rachel's hand. Then there was a pause which promised to become awkward, at which David said:

"Mother, I want to show you something in the back garden. You know I have been experimenting with my roses. I believe I have obtained some won-

derful color effects. You'll come also?" he asked
Rachel.

The three walked on together into the garden
where David exhibited and explained his work. When,
at length, Rachel said it was time she was going, the
mother urged her to come again.

"I'm going along with Sister Rachel to her home,
and to find out where she lives," explained David, as
he stepped along, unbidden, by Rachel's side.

And so these two walked side by side for the
first time. They talked freely on many topics, she
listening contentedly. They smiled into each other's
eyes, and at the end of that short journey, something had happened. True love had awakened in
two hearts. Through all the shifting scenes of
earth-life, nothing like this had ever come to this
man and this woman. Love had waited all this time.
The power that draws kindred souls together is not
limited to the few years of earth-life. While time
lasts, God will provide sometime, somewhere, in
which to give opportunity for every deserving soul.
Here were two whose hearts beat as one; but one
must needs have left mortality early in his course,
while the other went on to the end alone. The reason for this was difficult to see by mortal eyes, but
now—

"I'm coming again to see you," said David, as
he prepared to depart. "I have so much to tell you;
and you,—you have said very little. I must hear your
story too."

"I have no story," said she. "My earth-life was
very uneventful. I just seemed to be waiting—"

"Yes?"

But Rachel was confused. Her simple heart had spoken, and true to earthly habit, she now tried to cover up her tell-tale words; but he saw and understood, and as they stood there, his heart burned with a great joy.

"Good-bye," he said, as he took her hand, "may I come again soon?"

"Yes;" she answered. "I shall be pleased to see more of your beautiful flower garden."

This was the beginning of a courtship, not the less sweet because it had been postponed for so long; not the less real, from the fact that the man and the woman were spiritual beings. "Sin," said the apostle, "is without the body;" so love and affection are attributes of the spirit, whether that spirit is within or without a tabernacle of flesh. And this courtship did not differ to any great extent from all others which had taken place from the beginning of time. There were the same timid approaches and responses; the getting acquainted with each other, wherein each lover's eyes glorified every act in the other; the tremulous pressure of hands; the love-laden looks and words; the thrill of inexpressible joy when the two were together. Neither was this courtship exceptional. Among the vast multitude in the spirit world there are many who did not mate in the brief time allotted to them in the earth-life; therefore, congenial spirits are continually meeting and reading "life's meaning in each other's eyes."

Rachel, though she claimed to have no "story" to tell, interested David greatly in her account of how the Lord had chosen her as one of a family to become a savior on Mt. Zion. The work for the dead had not interested him. He, in connection with the youth of his time, had neglected that part of the gospel plan; and now, of course, he saw his mistake.

"Yes," David acknowledged to Rachel, "I see my error now, as usual, when it is too late to remedy it. You who were faithful rank above me here."

"Don't say that," she pleaded.

"But it is true. Your good deeds came before you here and gave you a standing. Some of the treasures you destined for heaven were detained here, and you are now reaping benefits from them. Do I not see it all the time? When we meet new people, you are received with delight—I am unknown."

"David, what comes to me, you partake of also, because—"

"Because you shall belong to me. Yes, dear one; that is the blessed truth. The Lord has brought us together, and all else should be forgotten in our gratitude to Him. . . . . Rachel, we would have known each other in earth-life had I behaved myself. Our lives were surely trending toward each other, and our paths would have met. We would have loved and have wedded there, had it not been for my—"

"Say no more. Let us forget the past in thinking of and planning for the future. I am happy now, and so is your mother."

"And so am I."

IV.

"Whatsoever God doeth it shall be forever."—*Eccl. 3:14.*

David and Rachel were out walking when they saw another couple whose lovelike actions were noticeable. As they met, the couple stopped and the man said, "Pardon me, but we are somewhat strange in this new world. May we ask you some questions?"

"Let us sit down here together," suggested David, and he led the way to a place where they could sit quietly. "Are you in trouble?"

"Well, I hardly know," replied the man. "Anna and I are together, and perhaps we ought to be satisfied; but somehow we are not. There is something lacking."

"Yes?"

"You see, we left the earth-life, so suddenly— we were so poorly prepared for this." His companion clasped his arm as if to be protected from some impending danger. "We were boating on the lake, the boat overturned, and here we are. . . . . We were to have been married the next day, but now— now what is our condition? We are not husband and wife; neither, I suppose, can we be, for we were taught back in that world from where we came, that there is no married condition here. Yet you two are husband and wife, are you not?"

"Not yet," replied David, "but we expect to be."

"I don't understand; you seem to know; teach us. May we be married here?"

David explained the principle of celestial marriage as it had been revealed to them in earth-life, and contrasted that doctrine with what was usually taught. "So you see," said he, "even if you had been married on that day appointed in mortality, it would have been only until death did you part. You have passed through death, and so, the contract between you would have come to an end, and you would not now be husband and wife."

"But you said that you two were to be married. How?"

"Had we been married in earth-life, it would have been for time and eternity, because it would have been performed by the authority of the Lord. What God does, is forever. Marriage must be solemnized on the earth. As our earth-days are past, we cannot go back, so the ceremony must be done for us by someone else living on the earth. Sister Rachel here, while in earth-life, did for thousands who had gone before what they could not do for themselves. Now, someone, in the Lord's own due time, will stand for her, and do for her what she did not do for herself."

The two new acquaintances listened attentively while David and sometimes Rachel instructed them on the principles of the gospel, and their application to those who were in the spirit world. They spoke to them of faith and repentance, principles which all men everywhere could receive and exercise. They explained the ordinance of baptism for the remission of sins, an earthly rite, which could be believed in and accepted by those in the spirit world, but would have to be performed for them vicariously by someone on earth. Marriage for eternity was also further explained.

"It is true," concluded David, "that in the resurrection there is neither marrying nor giving in marriage. All that must be attended to before the resurrection, which for all of us—luckily — is yet in the future. We know for a surety that if we do our part the best we know, the Lord will take care of the rest."

These four people did not part until David and Rachel had promised to meet their friends again soon, and continue the talk which had so favorably begun. When the two had left, David turned to Rachel and said:

"Did you see the lovelight glowing in their eyes when their hearts were touched with the truth?"

"Yes, as it did in yours when you were speaking."

"And in yours, too, my dear, when it was your turn."

"It's good to be a missionary—always a missionary, isn't it, as long as there is one being in need of guidance and instruction."

"It is very good, indeed, David."

"Rachel, glad news for us. We, you and I, are

soon to follow our parents and our older brothers and sisters, up through the gates of the resurrection, which our Lord so graciously opened. . . . . Yes, yes, it is true. . . . . Into the celestial kingdom, with bodies of celestial glory and go on to our exaltation. . . . . And, dear, the work is being done for us in the Temple of our God. . . . . Yes, right now, it is being done. Come, Rachel, let us go and be as near as we can. . . . . Yes, we have permission. . . . . This is the Temple. God's messengers are here, and His Spirit broods in and around the holy place. That Spirit we also in common with mortality, may feel. You, Rachel, ought to be at home here, more so than I. Let us follow the man and the woman who are doing the work for us. . . . . Do you see them clearly, Rachel? . . . . Yes; we shall not forget them when they, too, come to us in the spirit, but we shall give them a welcome such as they have never dreamed of. . . . . Now they are by the altar. Kneel here by me, Rachel,—your hand in mine, like this. Listen, can you hear? 'For and in behalf of,' . . . . you and me. . . . . It is done. We are husband and wife. You are mine for eternity, mine, mine. . . . . O, Eternal Father, we thank Thee!"

David holds the fair form of his wife in his arms. He kisses her cheeks, her eyes, her lips. Then there is silence.

PART FOURTH

Freedom waves her joyous pinions
  O'er land, from sea to sea,
Ransomed, righteous, and rejoicing
  In a world-wide jubilee.

O'er a people happy, holy,
  Gifted now with heavenly grace,
Free from every sordid fetter
  That enslaved a fallen race.

Union, love, and fellow feeling
  Mark the sainted day of power;
Rich and poor in all things equal,
  Righteousness their rock and tower.

Mountain peaks of pride are leveled,
  Lifted up the lowly plain,
Crookedness made straight, while crudeness
  Now gives way to culture's reign.

Now no tyrant's sceptre saddens:
  Now no bigot's power can bind.
Faith and work, alike unfettered,
  Win the goal by heaven designed.

God, not mammon, hath the worship
  Of His people, pure in heart:
This is Zion — oh, ye nations,
  Choose with her "the better part!"

Crown and sceptre, sword and buckler—
  Baubles!—lay them at her feet.
Strife no more shall vex creation;
  Christ's is now the kingly seat.

Cities, empires, kingdoms, powers,
  In one mighty realm divine.
She, the least and last of nations,
  Henceforth as their head shall shine.

'Tis thy future glory, Zion,
  Glittering in celestial rays,
As the ocean's sun-lit surging
  Rolls upon my raptured gaze!

All that ages past have promised,
  All that noblest minds have prized,
All that holy lips have prayed for,
  Here at last is realized.
                    —*Orson F. Whitney.*

I.

"Arise, shine; for thy light is come, and the glory of the Lord is risen upon thee. * * * And the Gentiles shall come to thy light and kings to the brightness of thy rising."—*Isaiah* 60:1, 3.

The sun in its downward course had reached the hazy zone, which, bounded by the clear blue above and the horizon below, extended around the green earth; in the west, the round disk of the sun shone through it, and tinged the landscape with a beautiful, mellow light.

It was midsummer. The sun had been hot all the day, and when on that evening two men reined in the horses they were driving, and paused on the summit of a small hill, a cool breeze reached them, and they bared their heads to the refreshing air. Not a word was spoken as they gazed on the scene before them; its grandeur and beauty were too vast for words.

Before them, to the west, lay the city, the object of their long journey—before them, it lay as a queen in the midst of her surroundings. At first sight, it seemed one immense palace, rather than a city of palaces, as the second view indicated. Street after street, mansion after mansion, the city stretched away as far as the eye could reach, mingling with trees and gardens.

Rising from the center of the city was the temple. Its walls shone like polished marble, and its towers seemed to pierce the sky, as around about them a white cloud hung. This cloud extended from the temple as a center, over the whole city, and seemed as it were a covering.

The sun sank behind the horizon; still the cloud glowed with light, as if the sun's rays still lingered there.

For ten minutes the carriage had paused on the elevation, and the two men had gazed in silence. Then the driver, as if awakening from a dream, gave the horses the word to go, as he said:

"We must drive on."

"Yes; night is coming on."

The second speaker was a middle aged man of commanding bearing. He leaned back in the carriage as they sped onward.

"So this is the world renowned city," he said, "the new capital of the world to which we all must bow in submission; within whose borders sit judges and rulers the like of which for power and wisdom have never yet appeared. Truly, she is the rising light of the world. What say you, Remand?"

" 'Tis indeed a wondrous sight, your majesty. The reality far exceeds any reports that have come to us."

"It is well, Remand, that we chose this slower mode of coming into the city. Electricity would have brought us here in a fraction of the time; but who would miss this beautiful drive?"

They were already within the outskirts of the city. Although all that day they had driven through a most beautiful region of cities and fields and gar-

dens, the latter being gorgeous with flowers and fruit,
yet the glory of this city far surpassed anything
they had yet beheld. Over the smooth, paved road-
way, their carriage glided noiselessly. The blooming
flowers and trees shed sweet odors in the air.
Buildings and gardens, arranged in perfect symmetry,
delighted the eye. The song of birds and the hum
of evening melodies charmed the ear. Men, women
and children and vehicles of all kinds were continually
passing.

The shades of night crept over the landscape; still
the cloudy covering of the city glowed with brilliant
light. The darker the night became, the brighter
became the cloud, until the palace, built of marble
and precious stone, appeared in its soft, clear light
like the colors of the rainbow.

"Your majesty, must we not soon seek some place
to rest for the night?"

"Yes, you are right. Do you think anyone will
suspect our true character?"

"No one save ourselves, within thousands of miles,
knows that you are the king of Poland."

"I do hope so, Remand, for I wish to see these
things from the point of view of a commoner. See,
there is the pillar of fire spoken about. Truly, my
good friend, the glory of the Lord is risen upon this
place."

Hardly were the words spoken before the carriage drew up to a gateway, or open arch, which
spanned the road. A man appeared and inquired of
the travelers where they were going. On being informed that they were strangers come to see the city,

the man bade them wait a few minutes. Soon he returned.

"As you are strangers and wish to rest for the night, you will please alight and receive that which you need. Your horses will be taken care of. Come." They drove along a road leading to a large house. Grooms took charge of the horses, and they themselves were ushered into a room, which, for convenience and beauty of finish, was not surpassed even by the king of Poland's own palaces. Soon fruits and bread were placed before them, and they were shown couches where they would rest for the night.

Though weary with their day's journey, the travelers could not sleep. The strangeness of it all bewildered them, and they talked about it far into the night.

Next morning they were awakened by song birds that had taken position in a tree near their open window, and were now pouring forth a chorus of welcome. How beautiful was the morning! Earth and sky were full of the perfume of flowers and the song of birds. The cloud still hung over the city.

From the garden they were called into the dining room, where a meal was spread before them. Fruits and fruit preparations of a dozen kinds; breads, cakes and vegetables, drinks from the juice of fruits: this was the bill of fare.

After they had eaten, the person who had met them the evening before, entered, and announced that their carriage was ready for their drive; or, if they chose to take the cars, they would get within the

city much quicker, but, of course, would miss some
interesting sights.

"We prefer to see all," replied the king.

"Then come with me."

The king and Remand followed into another room
where they met a young man who was to be their
escort. The first now retired, and the young man
advanced and shook their hands.

"Be seated for a moment," said he. "My name
is Paulus. I am to conduct you into the city, and be
your guide for the day. Such is the rule here." The
speaker also took a seat by the table. The king and
his companion sat opposite.

"In this city," continued Paulus, "there can be no
hypocrisy, no deceit of any kind. I am instructed,
therefore, to tell you that your true name, character,
and mission is known. You are the king of Poland,
and you his counselor and friend."

The king started, changed color, and looked towards Remand.

"How—how is that?" he stammered.

Paulus smiled. "Do not be alarmed, my dear
sir. You were known before you entered the first
gate yesterday. These people have entertained you
with a full knowledge of what you are; nevertheless,
the treatment you have received has been in no wise
different from that which is given to every honest
man who comes to this city for righteous purposes,
no matter be he high or low, rich or poor, in the
estimation of the world. You see, true worth and
righteousness are the only standards of judgment here.
Again, you are safer here than in the house of your

best friend in Poland, or surrounded by your old-
time host of armed warriors; for violence is no more
heard in this land, neither wasting nor destruction
within our borders. Our walls are Salvation; our
gates, praise; and the inhabitants of this city are all
righteous. It is their inheritance forever, for they are
a branch of the Lord's planting, the work of His hands,
wherein He is glorified."

Neither of the strangers spoke. The words seemed
to thrill them into silence.

"Come, then, let us be going."

The carriage was awaiting; but it was not the
travelers' own.

"No," was Paulus' answer to their inquiry, "your
horses will rest. This is our equipage."

They drove into the city.

" 'Walk about Zion, and go round about her; tell
the towers thereof. Mark ye well her bulwarks, consider her palaces, that ye may tell it to the generations
following,' " said Paulus.

"You quote from the writings of the ancient
Hebrews," said Remand.

"Yes; these 'holy men of God spake as they were
moved by the Holy Ghost,' " was the answer.

An hour's drive through indescribable grandeur
brought them to a gate in the wall which surrounded the temple, where they alighted. An attendant took charge of the horses. Paulus led the
way. A word to the keeper of the gate, and they
were permitted to pass. Surrounding the central
building, was a large open space laid out in walks,
grass plats, ornamental trees, and flowers. People

were walking about. Guides and instructors were busy with strangers, who seemed to have come from all nations, by the varied manner of dress displayed, and the different languages spoken.

"This," said Paulus, "is the sanctuary of freedom, the place of the great King. From this center go the righteous laws that govern nations and peoples. It is not time yet to proceed further, so we will walk about the gardens."

"Is the great King here today?" asked Poland's ruler.

"I do not know; but the council will sit and transact all needed business. And now I will tell you another thing: All whom you have met or seen have appeared to you as mortal beings, as you or I but in reality, in our drive through the city, you have seen many immortal, that is, resurrected, men and women; for you must remember that now the right eous live to the age of a tree, and when they die they do not sleep in the dust, but are changed in th twinkling of an eye. These visit with us, abide wit us for time to instruct us. Because you are a rule among the nations, you will be permitted to see th assembling of the council, and receive instructio from it. The time is drawing nigh. Let us be going

Great crowds of white-robed men were flockir into the temple. The three followed. The king ar Remand gazed in wonder at those who had bec pointed out as being resurrected beings, and the wonder increased when they could see no mark difference between them and the rest of mankir

save perhaps in the calm, sweet expression of the face, and the light which appeared to beam from the countenances of the immortals. They certainly were not unreal, shadowy beings.

Entering a wide hallway, they soon arrived at the council chamber. Its glory dazzled the beholders. In the midst of this room was a vast throne as white as ivory, and ascended by seventy steps. On each side of the throne were tiers of seats, rising one above the other. The seats were rapidly being filled, but the throne remained vacant.

"The King is not here today," whispered Paulus.

Then a soft, sweet strain of music was heard. It increased in volume until a thousand instruments seemed to blend into one melody. Suddenly, the vast assembly arose as one man and joined in a song of joy and thanksgiving.

"Guide—dear friend," whispered the king of Poland, "I am overcome, I cannot remain."

"I feel faint," said Remand, "I fear I shall perish."

"Come, then, we had better go," answered Paulus. "This is all we shall see at present. We shall now go into another room and wait the council's adjournment; then you will have an interview with one delegated to talk with you."

From the hallway they entered a smaller room, decorated with beautiful pictures and adorned with statuary. Books, newspapers and magazines were at hand, and when the visitors were tired of gazing, they sat down by a table.

They had not long to wait before word came

that the king and his friends should enter another room close by. Paulus would wait for their return. The two found a venerable looking man awaiting them, who, upon their entrance, arose and said:

"Welcome, welcome, to the Lord's house. I may not call you king of Poland—there is but one King on this earth—but I will call you servants of the King, as we all are. Be seated.

"I am instructed to tell you that, as a whole, the King is pleased with the manner you are conducting your stewardship. The Spirit of our Lord moved upon you to take this journey to his capital, and you chose to come as you did. That is well enough. Tyrants do not enter this city, and your presence here is assurance to you that you are justified.

"It is well that you have disbanded your armies, and that your instruments of war have been made into plows and pruning hooks. Remember the law that the nation and kingdom that will not serve the Lord shall perish. The King grants to all His subjects their free agency in the matter of religion, forcing no one to obey the gospel law; still He is the King of the earth; it is His, and He made it, and has redeemed it; and He now wills that all nations shall come under one government organized by Him in righteousness. For a thousand years the earth must rest in peace; then comes the great and dreadful day of the Lord.

"And now, another thing. There have been some complaints from your country that the servants of the Lord who have been sent to preach the gospel

to your people, have not had that perfect freedom
which is desired. Please see to it that they are not
molested while peaceably promulgating religious doctrines."

"I shall see to it," answered the king of Poland.

For some time they counseled together; then the
two withdrew, and joined Paulus, who conducted them
out into the city.

II.

"The wolf also shall dwell with the lamb, and the leopard
shall lie down with the kid; ° ° ° and a little child shall lead
them. They shall not hurt nor destroy in all my holy mountain
for the earth shall be full of the knowledge of the Lord as the
waters cover the sea,"— *Isaiah 11:6-9.*

The next day Paulus with his two visitors walked
about the city. He described and explained the many
deeply interesting scenes, and answered the numerous
questions directed to him. The foreigners did not
fail to note the wonderful advances made in the arts
and sciences and their practical application to every-
day affairs. They had thought their own country not
behind in improvements, but here their own were far
surpassed.

"We will ride out on the ether-line to one of our
schools," remarked Paulus. "You will be pleased with
the children."

"This is an improvement on electricity," said
their director, as seated in an elegant car, they were
carried through the city without noise or jostle.

"This line is rather crude yet. I was reading in the newspaper the other day that some very important improvements were shortly to be made. You have noticed, ere this, our method of heating and lighting. Don't you think it is an advancement on the old way?"

"It certainly is, though we use some steam and considerable electricity yet in our country."

"I suppose so — but here we are."

Although nothing in the city was cramped or crowded for room, the place where they now alighted was planned on an unusually large scale. Immense buildings stood upon a large tract of land, planted with trees, grass, and flowers. Here were breathing room and playground. A number of streams of clear water flowed through the grounds, and small ponds were alive with fish and swimming birds. Fountains played, and statues of marble gleamed through the foliage.

"See, what is that?" exclaimed Remand, as he caught sight of a huge, shaggy beast lying under a tree.

"Just a brown bear," said Paulus. "We have some lions and few of the rarest animals on these grounds — but I am forgetting that these scenes must be strange to you. In Poland you have not wholly shaken off the old world and its way. It takes time of course."

"Well," replied Remand, "although the enmity between man and beast is nearly gone, we have not yet adopted bears and lions as pets for our children to play with."

"Well, we have, you perceive."

A bevy of children came dancing through the grounds. Beautiful children they were, full of life and gladness. They caught sight of bruin, stretched under the tree, and with a shout they stormed him. The animal saw them coming, and extended himself at full length on the ground, seemed to enjoy the children's tumbling over his shaggy sides. When they patted him on the head and stroked his nose, he licked their hands.

"We haven't reached quite that far," remarked the king.

"Neither do we behold such sights," added his companion, as he pointed to a tiger crouching on the grass, and gazing with no evil intention at a lamb quietly feeding by.

"You will in time," said Paulus. "The earth is being filled with the knowledge of God. Hate, envy, and destruction are fast disappearing, and you see the natural results: the wolf lying down with the lamb, and children playing with once savage beasts. In this way, Satan is being bound, and the whole earth will soon be released from his power."

They came to another group of children, gathered on the shore of a small lake, who were eagerly listening to a man in their midst.

"We will hear what the lesson is today," said Paulus, and they went up to the group. The instructor was holding up a flower which he had plucked from the margin of the water, and was illustrating some peculiarity of vegetable formation to the class.

"It is botany today," said Paulus. "I hoped that it would be his favorite theme."

"And what is that?"

"The improvements on these grounds are the work of his planning and supervision, and he delights to give lessons on earth and water formations. He often sets a class to digging trenches and waterways. He says that he learned all about such things when he went to school, meaning when he was on the earth before."

"Is he a resurrected being?" asked Remand in a low voice.

"He is," was the reply. "Many of our instructors are. You will understand without argument the advantages they have over others."

"Certainly, certainly."

"I see he is through with the recitation. Let us speak to him."

As they came up, the children recognized them with a smile and a salute, and the instructor said:

"Welcome, brothers, welcome, Brother Paulus."

"You are dismissed. Go to your next lesson," he said to the children, and they quietly walked away.

"Now," said he, "I have some leisure. Will you all come with me into the reading room? I have something to show you, Paulus, and it may interest our visitors."

"Need we no introduction?" asked the king, as they followed into a large building.

"Not at all. He knows who you are."

The reading room was a compartment beautifully adorned and furnished. It was filled with tables, chairs, bookracks, etc. Hundreds of children were there reading. Perfect order reigned, though no overseers or watchers were seen. The three followed the instructor into a smaller room, seemingly arranged for private use. Chairs were placed, and then he opened a newspaper which he spread on the table.

"Have you seen the last edition of today's paper?"

None of them had.

"Well, I found something here of more than usual interest. It seems that some workmen, excavating for a building, came across the ruins of a nineteenth century city. In a cavity in a stone they found some coins of that period, also a number of newspapers. It was a common practice in those days to imbed such things in the corner stones of buildings. Extracts from those papers are reproduced here, and they are of interest to the children of today in showing the condition of the world when under the influence of that fallen spirit who rebelled against God in the beginning. Let me read you a few extracts, principally headings only."

" 'Yesterday this city was visited by a most destructive fire. One-half of the business part was swept away. Thousands of dollars of property were lost, and it is supposed that about fifty persons have perished in the flames.'

" 'The great strike. Thousands of workmen out of employment. Children crying for bread. Mobs march through the streets, defying the police, and demolishing property. The governor calls out the state militia.'

"Here is another:

" 'War! War! England, Germany, France, Russia and the United States are preparing!'

"Yes, you have read your histories. You know all about that. What do you think of this?"

" 'Millions of the people's money have been expended by those in office to purchase votes. A set of corrupt political bosses rule the nation.'

"Still another:

" 'A gang of tramps capture a train—' "

The reader did not finish, but laid the paper down and looked out of the open door. He did not speak for some time; then turning, said:

"Brothers, thank God that you live in the Millennium of the world. My heart grows sick when my mind reverts back to the scenes of long ago. I passed through some of them. I learned my lessons in a hard school; but God has been good to me. He has known me all along, and has given me just what I needed. Shall we visit the buildings? Shall we see the children who grow up without sin unto salvation? Come with me."

From room to room, from building to building, they went. Children, children, everywhere — bright, beautiful children. Oh, it was a grand sight! Hark! They sing — a thousand voices; and such music!

"Are there special visitors today?" asked Paulus.

"Yes; come let us go outside and see them."

They stepped out on to a portico where they could see the throng of children standing on a large lawn outside. They were singing a song of welcome, and through the trees could be seen three men approaching. The children made way for them, and they walked through towards the building.

"Look well at them as they pass," said the instructor; "you may recognize them."

They walked with the sprightliness of youth though their hair was white as snow. They smiled at the children as they passed.

"Two of the faces are familiar," remarked Remand, "but the third is strange. Surely, surely—"

"Surely you did not expect to see George Washington and Martin Luther in the flesh, walking and talking as other men?"

"Never."

"It is they."

"And the third?"

"The third is Socrates of old."

"What is their mission?"

"They are about to speak to the children. They have been at the school of the prophets all morning, and now they come from the high school yonder. You see what advantages today's students of history have."

"Has the knowledge of God exalted men to the society of resurrected beings?"

"Your senses do not deceive you," was the reply.

"Now I must go," said the instructor. "Farewell, and peace be with you."

He went into the house again, the three following directly, but they saw nothing more of him.

III.

"Every beast of the forest is mine, and the cattle upon a thousand hills ° ° ° for the world is mine, and the fulness thereof."—*Psalms 50:10, 12.*

The King of Poland and his counselor lodged that night in the city. Early next morning, Paulus came again for them.

"What do you wish to see, today?" he asked.

"Take us to some of your workshops and mills," replied the king; "we would like to learn more of your social and industrial conditions, about which we have heard."

A car soon took them to a part of the city where the work shops were situated. The buildings were not great, black-looking structures with rows of small windows in the walls; but they were handsome, spacious buildings, resembling somewhat the finest of the public buildings with which the visitors were acquainted in their own country. Remand noted the absence of smoking chimneys, and inquired about them.

"We have done away with all that," explained Paulus. "Pure air is one of the essentials to life. One of the crudest imperfections of the past was the wilderness of smoking chimneys which belched forth their blackness and poison into the atmosphere. As you have noticed, our city is clean, and the air above us is as clear as that above forests or fields."

"I suppose you use electricity for light and power," remarked Remand; "but you need heat, too."

"We use electricity for heat also," was explained. "We get it direct from the earth, also have it generated by water power, both from falls and the waves of the sea, and transmitted to us. Some of these power stations are hundreds of miles away among the mountains, and by the sea. We have also learned to collect and conserve heat from the sun; so, you see, we are well supplied for all purposes. This building," said the instructor, pointing to the one in front of which they had stopped, "is a furniture factory. Would you like to see it in working operation?"

"Yes; very much," said the king.

They entered clean, well-lighted, airy rooms where beautiful machinery was being operated by well-dressed and happy-looking workmen. The visitors passed from section to section, noting, admiring, and asking questions.

"Whose factory is this?" asked Remand of the guide.

"You mean who has charge — who is the steward?" corrected Paulus.

"No; not exactly that. This magnificent plant must have an owner, either an individual or a corporation. I asked for the ownership of the property."

The guide looked strangely at his companions.

Then he realized that these men had come from the parts of the earth where the celestial order had not yet been established. The old ideas of private property rights were still with them.

"My friends," he said, "the earth is the Lord's, and the fulness thereof. He is the only proprietor. How can weak, mortal man own any part of this earth! No, ownership is for a future time, a future state. Now we are only stewards over the Lord's possession."

"But someone must have charge here," said the king.

"Certainly. A master mechanic is steward over this factory, and he renders an account of all its doings to the Bishop, who is the Lord's representative. In this building, as you have seen, are many departments, and these are also stewardships, given to those in whose charge they are. Likewise, each workman has a stewardship for which he is responsible and accountable to the Lord."

They came to the wood-carving department where beautiful designs were being drawn and executed.

"Each man, as far as possible, does the kind of work best suited to his tastes and abilities. Here, for instance, those who are skilled carvers of wood find employment for their talent, and they turn out some fine articles of furniture. Of course, we have machines that stamp and carve wood; but the pleasure derived from the use of the skilled hand is not to be denied the well-trained mechanic and artist."

"I don't quite understand what you mean by

stewardships," said Remand as they passed into a
rest room.

"Let us sit down here," replied Paulus, "and I
shall try to explain further. You must know that
all this order, beauty, peace, and plenty has been
attained by an observance of celestial law. And the
celestial law as pertaining to temporal things is that
no man shall have more than is required for his and
his family's support. In this respect all men are
equal according to their needs. In olden times, this
law was called the order of Enoch, because we are
informed that Enoch and his city attained to a high
degree of righteousness through its observance.
Later it was called the United Order. It has been
revealed to and tried by men in various periods of
the earth's history, but never has it had such a
chance to redeem the world as it is having now.
According to this law, no man can accumulate unto
himself the wealth created by the work of others,
as was the case in former times with us, and still
prevails to some extent among other nations. All
surplus which a worker accumulates beyond his
needs is turned into the general storehouse of the
Lord. Thus each man becomes equal in temporal
things as well as in spiritual things. There is no
rich or poor: each man obtains what he requires,
and no more."

"What is the extent of this surplus?" asked the
king. "Is it large?"

"Yes; because of the nearly perfect condition
of our industrial system, a great amount of wealth
flows into the general storehouse. You will under-

stand, of course, that all public institutions receive
their support from this fund, so that the old order
of taxes is done away with. You have noticed our
beautiful city. You have not seen palaces of the
rich and hovels of the poor, but you have seen magnificent public buildings, parks, and thoroughfares.
These institutions that are for all alike have been
built and are sustained by the surplus; and this city
does not represent all of what the people of the Lord
are doing. The Lord's work is being extended
throughout this land and to lands beyond the sea.
Not the least of our duties is the building of temples
and the performing of the work for our dead in them.
So you see, we have need of much wealth to carry on
our work."

"Yes; I understand," remarked Remand; "but in
our country and time, as indeed, it has been in the
past, many have tried plans of equality, but they have
been more or less failures. Why have you succeeded
so well?"

"The chief cause for the past failures of the
world in this industrial order lies in the supposition
that unregenerated men, who have not obeyed the
gospel of Jesus Christ, and who are, therefore, full
of weaknesses and sins incident to human nature
without the power to overcome them — I say the mistake lies in the supposition that such men can come
together and establish a celestial order of things,
an order wherein the heart must be purged from
every selfish thought and desire. No wonder that
a building erected on such a poor foundation could
not stand. We have succeeded because we have

begun right. We have had faith in the Lord and His providences, have repented of our sins, have been born again of water and of the Spirit, and then we have tried to live by every word that proceeds from the mouth of God. We have done this pretty well, or we could never have succeeded in this work of equality that you see and admire. People who do the things that you observe around you must have the Spirit of God in their hearts. This celestial order is God's order, and those who partake of its blessings must be in harmony with God's mind and will. High law cannot be obeyed and lived by inferior beings who are not willing to submit to the first principles of salvation and power."

The three sat in quiet contemplation for a time. Then the king said: "Tell us about the wages of these workmen. The proper adjustment of wages has always been a source of much trouble with us."

"Yes, in the days when every man had to look out for himself and had no thought for his neighbor, it was a continual struggle to get as much as possible for one's work and to give as little as possible for the work of another. Such conditions were natural under a system of greed and selfishness, and they brought on much contention and trouble, which, happily are now ended. In the beginning," explained the speaker, "those who enter this order of equality are required to consecrate all their property to the Lord. Then each is given a stewardship according to his needs and his ability to manage and to work. Children have a claim upon their parents for support until they are of age, when they also are given a stewardship."

"Are the wages equal to all?"

"No; and for the very good reason that the needs of all are not alike. According to the old order, the superintendent of these works, for instance, would draw a salary of perhaps $5000.00 a year, while the men who do the manual labor would get less than a tenth of that sum."

"True," remarked Remand, "supply and demand regulates these things. Superintendents are scarce, but common workmen are plentiful."

"But, my dear friend, we have no common workmen. It is just as important that a table should be put together properly, and that it be well finished as that there should be a superintendent of the works. No man in our industrial system can say to another, 'I have no need of thee.' Each is important, each has his place, each supports the other. The polisher or the sawyer, therefore, should have his needs supplied, and so should the overseer — but no more. What would he do with more, anyway? Tell me."

"Why, why," replied Remand, "he could save it, put it in the bank, invest it."

Paulus smiled. "What good would hoarded wealth be to a man whose needs are all provided for as long as he lives, as also his children after him. We have but one bank here — the Lord's storehouse, and all profits derived from investments are there deposited. But speaking again of wages, I happen to know that the superintendent of this factory is a

man with a wife only to support, and they are very
simple in their tastes. The wood-carver whom we
spoke of has a large family of children. His needs
are greater than the superintendent's, therefore he
receives more for his portion. That is just, is it
not?"

"Yes," replied Remand, "the theory seems to be
all right but its application, among us at least, would
bring endless complications to be adjusted."

"Perhaps so," replied Paulus. "We are not perfect, even here. While we are in mortality, we have
weaknesses to contend with; but you must remember that we look on every man as a brother and a
friend, and as I have stated, we have the spirit of
the Master to help us. When this help proves insuf-
ficient by reason of our own failure to do the right,
and in our weakness we are unjust or over-bearing,
or oppressive, then there is the Lord Himself whose
throne is with us. He balances again the scales of
justice, and metes out to every man his just deserts."

Paulus arose, and the others followed him rever-
ently out into the park-like space surrounding the
factory. They walked slowly along the paths as they
talked.

"The argument usually urged against all orders
of equality," remarked Remand, "is that it takes away
man's incentive to work."

"Have you seen any idle men in or about Zion?"
asked the guide.

They acknowledged that they had not.

"The new order has not taken away incentives
to work; it has simply changed the incentive from

a low order to a higher. We can not afford to work for money as an end. Wealth, with us, is simply a means to an end, and that is the bringing to pass of saving righteousness to the race, individually and collectively. Wealth is not created to be used for personal aggrandizement; and, in fact, its power to work mischief is taken away when all men have what they need of it. The attainment of worldly wealth was at one time the standard of success. It was, indeed, a low standard."

"What is your standard?" asked the king.

"Among us the greatest of all is the servant of all. He who does his best along the line of his work, and contributes the results of his efforts to the general good, is successful. Quantity is not always the test, for the gardener who supplies us with the choicest vegetables is counted just as successful as he who digs from the mountain his thousands in gold. . . . Who, in your country, is counted the greatest success in history?"

Neither Remand nor the king replied to this query.

"I will not confuse you by urging a reply," said Paulus. "You, of course, understand our view of that matter. He who did the greatest good to the greatest number made the greatest success. That was the Lord and Master. 'If I be lifted up, I shall draw all men to me,' he said; and that is being fulfilled. In like manner the greatest among us is he who serves us best."

They seated themselves on a bench and watched

the workers flock from the workshop homeward to
their mid-day meal. It was an interesting sight to
the two visitors. The people appeared so happy and
contented that the king noticed it and commented
on it.

"Yes," replied Paulus; "why should they not be
happy? When I think of the times in the past — how
so many of the human race had to struggle desperate-
ly merely to live; how men, women and children
often had to beg for work by which to obtain the
means of existence; how sometimes everything that
was good and pure and priceless was sold for bread;
while on the other hand many others of the race
lolled in ease and luxury, being surfeited with the
good things of the world — I say, when I think of this,
I can not praise the Lord too much for what He now
has given to us."

"What are these men's working hours?" asked
Remand.

"The hours vary according to the arduousness of
the work, though it is now much more easy and pleasant, owing to our labor-saving machinery. From three
to four hours usually constitute a day's work. Some
prefer to put in their allotted time every day, and
then spend the remainder in other pursuits. Others
work all day, perhaps for a week, which would give
them a week to do other things. Others, again, who
wish more leisure for their self-appointed tasks, keep
steadily on for a year, thus earning a year for themselves."

"And what is done with this leisure?" asked the
king.

"Most of it is devoted to working in the temples
of the Lord, where the saving ordinances of the gospel
are performed for those who had not the privilege
to do them for themselves in this life; but many
other things are done. For instance, he who thinks
he is an inventor, devotes his time to perfecting his
invention; those who wish to pursue a certain line
of study, now have time to do so; some spend time in
traveling."

"Is there no competition among you?" said
Remand. "Such a condition, it seems to me, would
bring stagnation."

"We have the keenest kind of competition," was
the reply — "a competition of the highest order that
brings the most joyous life-activity into our work.
Each steward competes with every other steward to
see who can improve his stewardship the most and
bring the best results to the general storehouse. For
example, you noticed as you came into the city the
beautifully kept gardens and farms lying for miles
out into the country. These are all stewardships,
and there is the keenest competition among the farm-
ers and gardeners to see who can make the land
produce — first the best crops, and then the most of
that best. One man last year who has a small farm
turned into the storehouse as his surplus one thousand bushels of wheat. It was a remarkable record
which this year many others are trying to equal or
exceed. This sort of rivalry is found among all the
various businesses and industries in Zion and her
stakes; so you see, that even what you term the
wealth producing incentive is not lost to us, but is

used as an end to a mighty good, and not to foster personal greed."

The three strolled farther away from the large factory building, out into a section where residences stood here and there among the trees in the park-like grounds. Approaching a beautiful sheet of water bordered by flowering bushes, lawns, and well-kept walks, they saw a man sitting on a bench by the lake. As his occupation seemed to be throwing bread crumbs to the swans in the water, the king and his companion concluded that here, at last, they had discovered one of the idle rich, whom they still had in their own country. Remand expressed his thought to the guide.

"He idle?" was the reply. "Oh, no; he is one of our hardest working men. That is one of our most popular writers, and in many people's opinion, our best. We must not disturb him now, but we will sit down here and observe him. We are told that when he is planning one of his famous chapters of a story, he comes down to this lake and feeds the swans."

"And do you still write, print, and read stories?" asked Remand.

"Certainly. Imaginative literature is one of the highest forms of art. This man has most beautifully pictured the trend of the race, his special themes being the future greatness and glory of Zion. Why should he not paint pictures by words, as well as the artist who does the same by colors and the sculptor by form? If you have not read any of his books, you must take some of them home with you. See, he is moving away. Would you like to meet him?"

They said they would. The author was soon overtaken, and he received his visitors graciously.

"Yes," he laughingly acknowledged to Paulus, "you caught me fairly. I was planning a most interesting scene of the book on which I am now engaged, and the swans are a great help."

He led his visitors into the grounds surrounding his home, and then into his house. He showed them his books, his studio, and his collection of art treasures. From an upstairs balcony he pointed out his favorite bit of landscape, a mixture of hill and dale, shining water, and purple haze in the distance.

"Yes," he said, in answer to an inquiry, "I have read how, in former times, the workers in art, and especially the writer were seriously handicapped. The struggle for bread often sapped the strength which ought to have gone into the producing of a picture, a piece of statuary, or a book. Fear of some day wanting the necessities of life drove men to think of nothing else but the making of money; and when sometimes men and women were driven by the strong impulse of expression to neglect somewhat the 'Making a living,' they nearly starved. How could the best work be produced under such conditions? I marvel at what was done, nevertheless."

After spending a pleasant and profitable hour with the writer, the three visitors went on their way. They partook of some lunch at one of the public eating houses, then they went out farther into the country to look at the farms and gardens. Lines of easy and rapid transit extended in every direction, so that it took but a few minutes for Paulus and his friends to arrive at the place they desired. They alighted at an orchard, looked at the growing fruit and listened to the orchardist's explanations. After they had been left to themselves, Paulus continued:

"I want you to see and taste a certain kind of apple that this man has produced. Apples are his specialty." He led the way to another part of the orchard, and found a number of ripening apples which he gave his friends. "What do you think of them?" he asked.

"Most delicious!" they both exclaimed. "This might be the identical fruit that tempted Eve in the Garden of Eden," remarked Remand.

As they walked amid the trees, the conversation reverted again to the writer of books whom they had just left.

"This author's royalties must be very great —" began the king's counselor, and then checked himself when he remembered the conditions about him.

"Royalties?" replied Paulus; "yes, they are great; but they are not in money or material wealth. They consist in the vast amount of help, encouragement, hope, and true happiness he brings to his readers."

"But do not men like treasure for treasure's sake? Have your very natures changed?" asked the king.

"To some extent our natures have changed, but not altogether in this. Men and women still like to lay up treasures. It is an inevitable law that when men do some good to others, credit is given them for that good in the Book of Life. This wealth of good deeds may accumulate until one may become a veritable millionaire; and this treasure can never be put to an unrighteous use; moth can not corrupt it, nor thieves break through and steal."

"One more question," asked Remand. "I observed that your novelist had a beautiful house, many rare books, and some priceless paintings and pieces of sculptured marble. Are these among the 'needs' that you have spoken of so many times?"

"To him, certainly. Each man gets that which will aid him most in his particular line of work. Those things are not needless luxuries or extravagances. The writer is surrounded by beautiful things that he may be influenced by them to produce the most beautiful literature, just the same as any other laborer is provided with the best tools, helps, and environments that he may produce the best work."

From the orchard they went to the gardens and other workshops, closing the day with a visit to one of the large mercantile establishments of the city.

The next morning Paulus was on hand again to be their guide, but the king said:

"We must now return home. Much as we would like to remain — to take up our permanent abode here, I see that my duty calls me home. The Great King has something for me to do, and I shall try to do it. Let us be going."

Then the two visitors thanked their guide most graciously as he set them on their homeward way.

IV.

"In my Father's house are many mansions. * * * I go to prepare a place for you."—*John 14:2*.

Two men were walking in the grounds surrounding a stately residence on the outskirts of the city.

"I told you some time ago of the king of Poland's visit," said the one who had been instructor at the school. "Did you see that item in the paper this morning?"

"Yes," replied the other. "The visit must have made a great impression on him, judging by what he is doing."

"He was much interested. He is a good man, and is carrying out the instructions which he received while here. You have not been here before?"

"No; this is my first visit."

"This house is being built for a descendant of mine who is yet in mortality. I visit with him frequently, and he has asked me for suggestions as to its construction. I have had much pleasure in giving them. Soon he is to bring a wife into his new home, a dear good girl whom I am pleased to welcome in this way into our family. The workmen have nearly finished their labors and I am devoting some time to the preparation of the grounds. Will you have time to look around with me?"

"I have time today, brother."

They walked towards the house. It stood on the

slope of a gentle elevation which furnished a view of the country westward.

"Here you see what I am doing. I am departing somewhat from the usual form of lawn plans, but I want this place to have a special feature. You see, I have led this stream of water around the hillside and made it fall over this small precipice into this tiny lake. What do you think of it?"

"It is beautiful and unique."

"You see, brother, I have a liking for streams of water. They always please my eye, and their babble and roar is music to my ears. And then, someone else will soon be visiting with me here. I call this my temporary Earth-home; and brother, nothing can be too beautiful for my wife."

His companion looked at him and smiled. The speaker smiled in return. They understood each other.

"Yes, she is coming soon — at any time, now."

They walked into the house and inspected the building. It was no exception to the other houses in the city, as beautiful as gold, silver, precious stones, fine woods, silks, and other fabrics could make it. Most of the rooms were furnished, as if in readiness for occupancy.

"I delight in statuary," was explained to the visitor, "and my wife delights in paintings. You see, I have catered to both our tastes, and especially hers. Those panels are the work of the famous Rene, and this ceiling was painted by the best artist in the city. Here, what do you think of this?"

They paused before a large painting hung in the best light. It showed traces of age, but the colors indicated the hand of a master. It represented a scene where grandeur and beauty mingle; in the distance, blue hills; nearer, they became darker and pine clad; in the foreground loomed a rocky ledge; encircled by the hills, lay a lake, around whose shores were farms and farm houses with red roofs; and in the foreground of the lake was an island.

"A fine picture," said the visitor, "and an old one."

"It is a scene in old-time Norway, by one of Europe's best painters. Here is another. This is new, hardly dry, in fact.. You observe that there are no pines on those hills. The farm house and the orchard in the foreground are as natural as life. She will recognize them at once."

They passed out.

"I have not had time to collect much in the way of statuary. I work a little at that art myself. Here is an unfinished piece, a model for a fountain."

They sat on a bench within sight of the falling water.

"Tell me about your family."

"I have a wife and four children yet in the spirit world. It is not long as we count time since I left them, and they are soon to follow; but I am impatient, I think. Oh, but she is a good woman, brother, good and true and beautiful; and my children are noble ones — two boys and two girls — even if one has been wayward. He will come back in time. Yes, my wife first taught me the knowledge of God, in the second estate, and opened to me the beauties of our Fathers' great plan. I had fallen low, and was in

danger of going lower, when she came — God sent
her — and with her pure, strong hand drew me up from
the mire, God bless her." And the speaker smiled at
the splashing waters.

"Then in earth-life I left them so suddenly, and
she struggled bravely on to the end. It was all for
the best — we know that now. I had a work to do
in the spirit world, and God called me to it. I did it,
and was accepted of the Master. We all met in the
spirit world, and there continued our labors of love
for the glory of God and the salvation of His children.
Then my time came to pass through the resurrection,
and here I am. — Hark, what is that? Someone is
calling."

They listened. From the house came a voice, a
low, sweet voice, calling.

"Brother, I must go," said he who had been talking. "Someone calls my name."

He disappeared hurriedly within the doorway;
and the visitor went on his way.

V.

"And God shall wipe away all tears from their eyes; and
there shall be no more death, neither sorrow, nor crying, neither
shall there be any more pain: for the former things are passed
away.

"He that overcometh shall inherit all things; and I will
be his God and he shall be my son."—*Rev. 21:4-7.*

A sound, a whispered word echoes through the
air and enters the ear. It touches the chords and
finds them tuned to its own harmony. It plays ten-

derly on responsive strings, and what an awakening
is within that soul! What rapture in the blending,
what delight in the union! From it is born a joy of
the heavenly world.

A sight, a glimpse of a form – a certain form or
face; the rays of light entering the eye meet with
something keenly sympathetic, and the soul leaps in
ecstasy.

A touch, a gentle pressure of the hand; the union
is complete.

What was that voice that reached him – a voice
love-laden, full to overflowing from the regions of the
past? Ah, what sweetness courses through his veins,
what joy leaps in his heart!

Within, he sees her. She stands in the middle of
the room, with her eyes upon the open door. She
does not move. Her beautiful robe of shining white
clings about her form or falls in graceful folds to
the floor. Her hair, light as of old, now glistens like
silken threads. Her face shines with the indescribable
glow of immortality.

She sees her husband. She raises her arms, and
takes a step forward. She smiles – such a smile!

"Homan – Rupert."

"Delsa – Signe."

He takes her in his arms. He kisses her and holds
her to his breast. . . . .

Presently strains of music came from another
room. He listened as if surprised, but she looked up
into her husband's eyes and smiled. The music ceased
and a little girl appeared in the doorway.

"May I come in?" she asked.

"Alice, my darling."

She runs towards them.

"Papa, papa, oh, how glad I am!"

He lifted her up and she threw her arms about his neck and kissed him again and again.

"What a beautiful place this is!" she said. "O, mamma, I am very happy!"

"Yes, Alice, we are all happy — happy beyond expression. We now can partly understand what glorious truth taught us, that 'spirit and element, inseparably connected, receiveth a fulness of joy.'"

.   .   .   .

Alice was playing with the fishes and the swans in the garden, and the husband and wife were sitting by an open window, gazing out upon the city.

"Brother Volmer has not been to see us yet," said he. "You remember he was our brother Sardus?"

"I remember him well," she answered.

"His musical talent is now of great blessing to himself and to the cause of God, as he is a musical director in the Temple. He understands now why he lost his hearing while in mortality, and he praises God for his then seeming misfortune."

"Husband," said she, "I am thinking again about our children. How long will it be before we shall receive them all?"

"Not long now; but each in his order. Leave that to the Lord."

They looked out at Alice. The swans were eating from her hand, and she was stroking their curved necks.

"To look back," said he, "and see the wonderful

ways through which the Lord has brought us to this
perfection, fills my heart with praise to Him. Now
we are beyond the power of death and the evil one.
Now the pure, life-giving spirit of God flows in our
veins instead of the blood of mortality. Now we can
know the two sides of things. We understand the
good, because we have been in contact with the evil.
Our joy is perfect, because we have experienced pain
and sorrow. We know what life is, eternal life, because
we have passed through the ordeal of death."

"Yes, Father teaches a good school."

"And we have learned this truth," said she, "that
existence itself is a continuous penalty or reward.
The children of God reap as they sow from eternity
to eternity."

"Yes; then dwell on this thought for a moment:
Our lives have just begun, as it were. We have
eternity before us, and we are only now equipped
to meet it."

"I am lost in the thought. But tell me about
this thousand years of earthly peace and the last great
change. Husband, I am a pupil now, and you the
teacher."

"There is much to tell in contemplating not only
the realities but the possibilities of the future. This
earth has for some time been enjoying its Sabbath
of peace and rest. He who rebelled in the beginning
and fought against God is bound, and Christ is sole
King of the earth. His laws go to the ends thereof,
and all nations must obey them. The Saints are
building holy places, and working for the living and
the dead. No graves are now made, as the bodies of

the Saints do not sleep in the dust. Thus it will go
on until the thousand years are ended. Then Satan
will be loosed for a little season; but his time will be
short. Then comes the last great scene. The Lord
will finish His work. In the clouds of heaven, with
power and great glory, He will be seen with all His
angels. The mortal Saints yet on the earth will be
instantly changed and caught up to meet Him. The
holy cities will be lifted up. Then the elements will
melt with fervent heat. The earth will die as all
things must, and be resurrected in perfection and
glory, to be a fit abode, eternally, for celestial beings.
All things will become new; all things will become
celestial, and the earth will take its place among the
self-shining stars of heaven. Then shall we receive
our eternal inheritance, with our children and our
families. Then shall we be in possession of that better
and more enduring substance spoken of by the prophets. All things shall be ours, 'whether life or death, or
things present, or things to come;' all are ours, and
we are Christ's and Christ is God's."

"Why, then we will be like unto God."

"And is it strange that children should become
like their father?"

"I remember now," said she, "as distinctly as
though it were yesterday, what Father promised us
in our first estate, that if we were faithful, we should
be added upon, and still added upon. Do you remember it?"

"Distinctly," he answered. "It was to be 'glory
added upon our heads for ever and ever.' Father is
fulfilling his promise."

Then they sat still, not being able to speak their thoughts, but looked out towards the cloud-encircled towers of the city.

Alice came running in. "The people are coming," she said.

They looked out of the window and saw two persons approach, viewing the grounds with interest.

"It is Henrik and Marie," exclaimed Signe. The newcomers were greeted rapturously.

"Come in and see the results of my husband's planning," said Signe.

The visitors were led through the house, and shown the gardens surrounding it. As they had been separated for a time from their friends they had many things to tell each other.

"Do you know," said Henrik, as they were all sitting by the playing fountain, "on our way here, we met Rachel!"

"Is she also risen?" asked Signe. "Oh, why did you not bring her with you?"

"Well," said Henrik with a smile, "I told her where we were going and asked her to come along. But she naturally preferred to stay with her husband who was taking her to see some of his own people; so she graciously declined, but said she would visit with us some other time."

"Right away?"

"I can't say. She clung pretty closely to her husband. They are a splendid pair. I am glad, for I will admit that I once thought Rachel's case was hopeless."

"We couldn't see very far, could we, brother?" remarked Rupert.

"Our faith was weak, and we did not trust the Lord enough."

"Yes; I used to wonder how the Lord would ever straighten out the mass of entanglements that seemed to exist in the world. We failed to comprehend the providences of the Lord because we could not see beyond the narrow confines of the world in which we were living; we could see only a small part of the circle of eternity; we could not see how that visible portion, which was often rough and unshapely, could fit into anything beautiful; but now our vision is extended, and we have a larger, and therefore, a more correct view."

"And this I have found," said Henrik, smiling at Signe and Marie as with arms around each other, they sauntered down the garden path, "I have found that our work never ends. While in earth-life my mission was to seek after those of my people who had gone before me, and to do a work of salvation for them in the temples. In the spirit world, I continued my work preaching to my fellowmen, and preparing them to receive that which was and is being done for them by others. And now, I find, that I am busier than ever. We are teachers, directors, leaders, judges, and our field is all the earth."

"Yes," replied Rupert, "I attended the laying of the cornerstone of the one hundredth temple the other day; and we have only just begun. The time, talent, wealth, and energy that formerly went to the enriching of a few and that was spent to build and

sustain armies and navies, now are directed to the
building of temples and the carrying on the work in
them. I used to wonder how the needed temple work
could ever be done for the millions of earth's inhabitants, but now I can see how simple it is. Tens of
thousands of Saints, in thousands of temples, in a
thousand years of millennium can accomplish it.
Every son and daughter of Adam must have a
chance; every tangled thread must be straightened
out; every broken link must be welded; every wrong
must be righted; every created thing that fills the
measure of its creation must be perfected; — all
this must be before the 'winding-up scene' comes.
All this can be accomplished, for now we have every
force working to that end. The earth is yet teeming
with our brothers and sisters in mortality; there is
continual communication between the spirit world
and this world, and then here are we, with our kind;
we have passed through the earth-life, through the
spirit world, through the resurrection — and we, as
you said, are busier than ever, because with our added
knowledge and wider view comes greater power.
Our services are needed everywhere. And what a
blessed privilege we have in thus being able to help
the Lord in the salvation of His children and the
hastening to its destined end of celestial glory this
world of ours."

Alice was playing with some birds, which she
seemed to have well trained, as they were flying back
and forth from her hand to the bushes. The two
women now came back along the path, stopping now

and then to listen to a bird or to look at a flower. They joined Rupert and Henrik.

"I have quite a lot of names from the spirit world to bring to the Temple today," said Rupert, "among them fifteen couples to be made husband and wife."

"I have heard it said," remarked Marie, "that in heaven there is neither marrying nor giving in marriage."

"Neither is there," answered Rupert, "any more than there is baptism for the remission of sins. Neither this world nor the world of spirits, where live the contracting parties, is heaven."

"Isn't this heaven?" asked Marie, looking around on the beauty with which she was surrounded.

"As far as we resurrected beings are concerned," replied Rupert, "we have heaven wherever we go; but this earth is only being prepared for its heavenly or celestial state. Until that is finished, there shall be marrying and giving in marriage."

"I'm glad of it," said Signe; "for there is —"

She was interrupted by Alice, who came in with the announcement that others were coming up to the house. Henrik and Marie were greeted for the first time by visitors who continued to gather. For some time, white-clothed persons had been directing their steps towards the Temple. Now they were hurrying.

"It is time to go," said Rupert.

In a few moments they had changed their clothing and with the speed of thought, they were within the Temple grounds. Entering, they took their places.

Volmer passed, and he paused to speak to them. Soon the hall was filled.

The Lord of Life and Light was there, and lent of His light to the scene.

Brilliancy pervaded everything, shone from everything. It was not the sun, there being no dazzle; it was not the moon, but a clearness as of noon-day. The whole Temple shed forth a lustre as if it were built of some celestial substance. The marble, the precious stones, the gold, seemed changed into light — light, pure, calm, and consolidated into form. It radiated from the throne, and from Him who sat upon it. "Around His head was as the colors of the rainbow, and under His feet was a paved work of pure gold in color like amber."

Hark! the music! How it fills the Temple, how it thrills the souls assembled. A thousand instruments blend in exquisite harmony, ten thousand voices join in the song:

> "The earth hath travailed and brought forth her strength,
> And truth is established in her bowels;
> And the heavens have smiled upon her;
> And she is clothed with the glory of her God;
> For He stands in the midst of His people.
> Glory, and honor, and power, and might
> Be ascribed to our God; for He is full of mercy,
> Justice, grace, and truth, and peace,
>   Forever and ever, Amen."

PART FIFTH

The rise of man is endless. Be in hope.
All stars are gathered in his horoscope.
The brute man of the planet, he will pass,
Blown out like forms of vapor on a glass.
And from this quaking pulp of life will rise
The superman, child of the higher skies.
Immortal, he will break the ancient bars,
Laugh and reach out his hands among the stars.

—Edwin Markham

I.

Old things have passed away, all now are new;
Its measure of creation Earth has filled;
The law of a celestial kingdom it
Has kept, transgressed not the law;
Yea, notwithstanding it has died, it has
Been quickened once again; and it abides
The power by which that quick'ning has been done
Wherefore, it now is sanctified from all
Unrighteousness, and crowned with glory, e'en
The presence of the Father and the Son.

Immortal Earth on wings of glory rolls,
Shines like unto a crystal sea of glass
And fire, whereon all things are manifest:
Past, present, future, — all are clear to those
Who live upon this glorious orb of God.

Upon this globe, God's children glorified
Are no more strangers, wand'ring to and fro
As weary pilgrims; now they have received
Possessions everlasting on the Earth —
A portion of a glorified domain
On which to build and multiply and spread —
A part of Earth to call always their own.
Eternal mansions may they now erect;

Make them of whatsoe'er their hearts' desire;
For gold and silver, precious stones and woods,
And fabrics rare, and stuffs of every hue,
All plentiful in Nature's store-house lie,
For them to freely draw upon and use.
Masters of all the elements are they;
And Nature's forces are at their command.

The man and woman, in the Lord made one,
Eternally are wedded man and wife.
These now together make their plans, and build
A lovely, spacious home wherein to dwell,
A place for work, for rest, for new-found joys,
A peaceful habitation, one beyond
The power of evil ever to destroy.

II.

In their primeval childhood — first estate —
These once had lived within their Father's home.
Out from that home they had been sent to Earth
To have their spirit bodies clothed upon
With element, to come in contact with
Conditions which were needful for their growth,
And learn the lessons of mortality.
There they had overcome temptation's wiles,
There had obeyed the gospel of their Lord
And worked out their salvation by its power.

These two had met and mated, had fulfilled
The first great law: "Give bodies clean and strong

To Father's spirit-children from above."
The time allotted they had lived on Earth,
Had died the mortal death, had gone into
The spirit world; from there they had come forth
With resurrected bodies from the grave.
Thus they had kept their first and second estates
And now were counted worthy to receive
Their portion 'mong the exalted ones of God.

III.

Celestial man and woman now do live
The perfect life; for every faculty
Of heart and brain is put to highest use.
The appetites and passions purged are
From dross that fallen nature with them mixed.
The will is master now, and every sense
Is under absolute control, and gives
Perfected service to perfected souls.

These two have come into their very own.
They walk by sight; and yet the eye of faith
Sweeps out to future time and distant space
And leads them on and on. They lay their plans
And execute these plans to perfectness.
Eternal Glory-land is their abode,
So beautifully clothed in Nature's best,
And basking in the pleasing smile of God;
No need of light of sun or moon or stars;
The glory of the Father and the Son
Eclipses all such lights of lesser ray.

Although with godlike powers they rule and reign,
Yet are they Father's children, and to Him
All loving honor and obedience give.
And then that Elder Brother who has done
So much for all, He also here abides,—
The Savior of the world and souls of men,
The Lord of lords, the King of all the Earth,
Yet ever-present Comforter and Friend.

IV.

And now they learn the things they could not know
On mortal earth. They learn the secrets of
All things are in space above, or in
The Earth beneath: the elements which form
The air that man did breathe, and where obtained,
And how composed. They learn of primal rocks,
Foundations of the new-formed worlds in space,
And how these worlds evolve into abodes
For man. The source of light and heat and power
They find, and grasp the laws by which they may
Be rightly used and perfectly controlled.
And then, most precious gift! they learn of life:
What makes the grass to grow, what gives the flowers
Their fragrance and their many-colored hues.
They comprehend all life in moving forms,—
In worm, in insect, fish, and bird, and beast;
And knowing this, they have the power to draw
Life from its store-house, and to make it serve
The highest good in never-ending ways.

V.

The truth has made these holy beings free.
They having overcome all evil powers,
Unfettered now they are and free to go
Where'er they wish within the heavenly spheres.
They're not alone on this perfected world,
Here other children of the Father dwell,
Who also have obeyed celestial law.
All these are of the Father's household, and
Are numbered with the just and true, of whom
'Tis written, "They are God's," and they shall dwell
Forever in the presence of their God.

What bliss to mingle with such company!
To taste the joys of friendships perfected,
And to feel to fulness that sweet brother-love
Which binds in one the noble race of Gods!

And other worlds may now be visited;
For end there's none to matter and to space.
Infinitude holds kingdoms, great and small,—
Worlds upon worlds, redeemed and glorified,
And peopled with the children of our God,
Who also have evolved from lower things.
What opening visions here for knowledge rare!
What sciences, what laws, what history!
What stories of God's love in other worlds!
Exhaustless themes for poets' sweetest songs;
For painters, sculptors, every science, art
Has never-ending fields of pure delight.

To them "the universe its incense brings"—
Distilled from all the sweetness of the spheres.

VI

Earth's loveliest flow'r, the love 'tween man and **wife**
Transplanted is to this most holy sphere.
Through all the toiling years of earth-life, it
Had grown; and now, instead of dying with
The mortal death, its roots are firmly fixed
In the eternal soil of Glory-land.
And blessed man! now at his side there stands
A woman, one of heaven's queens, a wife,
A mother to his children of the Earth,
And yet to be a mother of a race.
Her beauty rare surpasses power of words.
Her purity, her sweetly gentle ways
Rest as a crown of glory on her brow.
Her love transcendent fills his heart with joy,
And now he fully realizes that
"The woman is the glory of the man."

Here in thy Home, O Woman all divine,
Thy measure of creation thou doest fill!
Intelligences come from out the womb
Of Time, into thine own; thence are they born
With spirit bodies, to thy loving care.
Now thou art Mother, and doest know in full
A mother's joy — a joy untinged by pain,
And with thy Husband thou hast now become
Creator, fellow worker with thy Lord.

ial Father, Mother at the head
parentage they stand, the perfect type
that eternal principle of sex
ound in all nature, making possible
For every living thing to multiply
And bring increase of being of its kind.
In this celestial world, the fittest have
Survived. To them alone the pow'r is given
To propagate their kind. 'Twas wisely planned.
The race of Gods must not deteriorate.
Thus everlasting increase is denied
To those who have not reached perfection's plane.
Herein is justice, wisdom all-divine,
That every child born into spirit world
Has perfect parentage, thus equal chance
Is given all to reach the highest goal,
And win the race which runs up through the worlds.

And children fill the household of these Two —
And children bring perpetual youth, renew
The tender sentiments, and firmly knit
The heart of Father, Mother close in one.
Thus do they work, and thus they follow in
The footsteps of their Father; and they spread
Out o'er the land of their inheritance.
Masters of all, joint owners of the spheres,
Eternal increase of eternal lives
Is theirs; and this their work and glory is
To bring to pass the immortality
And life eternal to the race of men.

VII.

Time passes as an ever-flowing stream.
The many mansions teem with offspring fair,—
The spirit children of this heavenly world.
Varied are they, as human beings are
In form, in likes, in capabilities.
Here love, combined with justice, rules;
Here truth is taught, the right and wrong are shown;
Yet agency is given all, and they
May choose the way selected by desire.
Thus some more faithful are than others, and
Advanced more rapidly along the great
Highway that leads among the shining stars.

Time passes,— and the time has fully come
When spirits must be clothed upon with flesh,
Must follow in the footsteps of their Sire,
Must go to mortal earth and there work out
Their soul's salvation in the self-same way
That all perfected beings once have done.

Far out in space where there is ample room
And where primeval element abounds,
This Father has been working, and still works,
Fashioning a world on which to place
His children. Without proper form, and void,
In the beginning, this new world has passed
From one stage to another, until now
It rolls in space, an orb in beauty clad,
A world on which a human race may dwell.

This Father to his children thus doth speak:
"The time has come for you to leave this home —
This first estate, and take another step
Along progression's path. A new-formed world
Is ready to receive you, and to clothe
You in another body. You will then
Learn many things you cannot here receive.
A veil will then be drawn before your eyes
That you will be unable to look back
To us. Alone you'll have to stand; be tried
To see if faithful you will still remain.
There's darkness in that world; and sin will come
And pain and suffering such as now you know
Not of. But these will only clearly show
How good is righteousness, and how much more
To be desired the light than darkness is.
Yet, you shall not be wholly left alone;
My ministering angels shall keep watch,
And near you all the time my power shall be,
To help you in your direst hours of need.
My sons and daughters, as you now do live
Within your Father's ever-watchful care,
Know this that always shall his loving arm
Extended be to you; the Father-heart
And Mother-heart eternally do yearn
And feel for you in sorrow or in pain.
Where'er you are, you're still within my reach.
If you'll but turn to me, I'll hear your cries
And answer you in my good time and place.
Go forth as you are called, the lessons learn
Of earthly school; fear only sin; abide

By law, nor seek to be a law unto
Yourselves, for by eternal law the worlds
Are formed, redeemed, and brought to perfectness,
Together with all flesh which on them live.
Go forth. Be worthy to come back again
And be partakers of all heights and depths,
Things present, things to come, yea, life or death,
And it shall be my pleasure to bestow
Upon you *all there is eternally.*"

Joy fills this Father's children, and with one
        United voice of gladness do they sing:
"Thanks, Father, kind and good for what you've done;
        Thanks for the added blessings which you bring.
O glorious, wond'rous truth that we have found:
        The course of Gods' is one eternal round!"

THE END